THE COLLAPSE: FIVE MINUTES TO MIDNIGHT

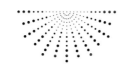

PENELOPE WRIGHT

For CarrieAnn Brown

CHAPTER ONE

July 6, 2018 – Rosie

"Carlos!" Jordan yells. "Get Rosie in the tent!"

People jump up and clear a path as Carlos wraps his arm around my waist and helps me across the campsite and into the tent we're borrowing.

Jordan hurries along beside us. "You must have had a seizure." She twists her hands together in front of her body. "Get her in there so she can lie down and have some privacy," she says in a low tone to Carlos.

My teeth chatter, but I don't feel cold.

"Oh my god. Wrap her in a blanket. I think she's in shock," Jordan says.

I am in shock, but not the kind she thinks.

Carlos nods tersely and tucks a blanket around my shoulders. "I'm going to find you some food," he says. "We need to get your blood sugar up." He crawls out and lets the tent flap fall shut behind him, and I'm plunged into murky gray darkness.

Minutes ago I was sitting by the fire at a homeless encampment deep inside Scriber Lake Park where Carlos and I are staying the night, and I'd just achieved this strange state of hopeless peace. I've been stuck here in 2018 for nearly a month with no way to get home.

When my stepmother tried to murder me in 2074, my only escape was into the past via a syringe of time travel chemicals I had hidden in my vest pocket. In my own time, I was deep underwater and on the verge of drowning. That same spot in 2018 is where Carlos lived in a tent on the streets of Seattle. I must have appeared several feet aboveground because I fell on top of Carlos's tent in the middle of the night on June 19th of this year. I was soaking wet and had no memory of who I was or where I was from. Carlos watched out for me until I passed out from a raging infection and he took me to the hospital.

Strong antibiotics and anti-radiation medicine brought me back from the brink of death, but when I regained my memories I realized I was still teetering on the cliff's edge of disaster. We all are. Me, Carlos, everyone in this camp, and the seven billion other people on the planet. We're only months away from The Collapse.

Early next year, the entire continent of Antarctica will flash melt and the sea level will rise two hundred feet overnight. I'm one of the few thousand survivors living in The United Towers, scratching out an existence above the flood line on the top floors of Seattle skyscrapers.

I've been trying desperately to figure out a way to get home, to escape what I know is coming.

"Rosie?" Carlos pushes aside the tent flap and crawls inside, the weak beam of a flashlight guiding his way. It's still dark in here, but now I can see the concern in his warm, brown eyes. "I found you a banana." He extends the yellow fruit toward me. "That will help with the leg cramps too."

"Thank you." Gripping the banana, I ease down the peel. I take a bite and Carlos squeezes in next to me, wrapping his arm around my waist. I lean my head against his shoulder and he kisses the top of my head.

I haven't only been trying to save myself, either. I'm not leaving Carlos here to die. A piece of the banana sticks in my throat and I swallow hard. Ever since I regained my memories, I've wrestled between two extremes. On the one hand, I've been terrified and desperate, searching for a way to contact my father, to get the time travel chemicals I need for both Carlos and me to escape to 2074. On the other hand, I've experienced more joy and happiness than I've ever known. The feelings that course through me when I'm around Carlos, when I look at him, when I hear him breathe. I think that's called falling in love.

I must save him. I don't want to imagine my life without him at this point. He's coming with me to 2074. There is no acceptable alternative. And it's not like The Towers offer total safety or any sort of comfort, but staying here is certain death.

Or at least I thought it was. Now I'm not so sure.

I need time travel chemicals to return to 2074, but the only person who can bring them to me is my father. But my dad doesn't know what year I'm in. He might not even know I'm lost in the past at all. I tried to send him a message, but the communication system we use to send notes from the past to our own present day was stolen or sabotaged. There's no point in me replacing the missing box with another. It would just get snatched again, and it would send a signal to whoever took the box in the first place that I don't want to send. It kills me though, because for all I know, Dad thinks I'm dead.

My father, David Columbia, is the president of our world, and he's a time traveler like I am. I had one final plan to contact him, and it seemed like a good one. I would find my grandmother in this time. Dad loved his mother more than anyone. She died in 2057, almost a year before I was born, and when she died, Dad transferred all that love to me. I was named after her. She's the one who had the foresight to plan for the coming disaster and save humanity from extinction.

My grandmother was supposed to be a teenage girl right now. I thought if I could find her, I could find my dad. Because if he can travel through time and he can't find me, wouldn't his next logical step be to find his mother? If I could locate her, maybe it would lead me to him.

But I just figured something out. Something terrible, and incredible, and utterly impossible, but nevertheless true. My grandmother is me.

In less than a year it will be me who adopts my father as an infant, not a fantasy grandmother who never existed.

Carlos and I were just sitting around the campfire and I'd been feeling unbelievably calm and serene. I guess when you finally lose all hope, you find your hollowness replaced by a strange peacefulness. At least that's what happened to me. I'd accepted it. And then…

The conversation wandered. We talked about all sorts of things. Then a girl went on a tangent about spiders. How great they were, how misunderstood, how nutritious.

And I'd gone into convulsions. My head felt like it was splitting in two as I was flooded with new memories. Memories of the thousands of spider carcasses I've eaten over the years. Memories of the spider farm floors. I've inspected them. I've helped solve problems. I've even helped clean up after a few big escapes.

But until that girl uttered those fateful words none of it had happened before. I was assaulted by an onslaught of all new memories of things that I'd grown up with, which didn't occur until the girl standing by the campfire with her hip cocked, rhapsodizing about spiders, had put the thought in my head.

When my 'seizure' ended. I'd grown four inches and gained I don't know how much weight. My hair is longer. My fingernails are stronger. My teeth even feel different inside my own mouth —smoother, thicker.

And I know. I know what happened. We didn't grow spiders before because I hadn't learned about it yet. But now that I have, it's part of our collective experience. One of our tools for surviving until the Earth recovers and we can retake the planet.

We know about it because I know about it. Because I am Rosarita Columbia. I am my father's daughter, and his mother. He just hasn't been born yet.

I cannot escape this world. I am the one who creates it.

There is no future without me.

CHAPTER TWO

July 6, 2018 – Ellen

I slouch in my camp chair at the back of my tent in The Jungle, the homeless encampment under the elevated section of Interstate 5 in South Seattle. I flip my knife end over end in my hands. The warm night feels muggy. Even after more than a year of living here in pre-Collapse Seattle, it sometimes feels weird to be outside the protection of Tower walls, exposed to unfiltered air.

Rosie's out there too, somewhere in the night, with Carlos. And I will find them. There have been so many false alarms. So many people trying to curry favor, feeding me old useless information…guesses…outright lies. I've seen through them all.

It's goddamn July 6th. I don't have time to dick around. How could someone like Carlos simply vanish into thin air? Now there's another one here outside the tent, checking in with my door guard, says she has 'information to share.' It's going to be another waste of my time, I'm sure, and I am in no mood.

I hear the unmistakable sound of a thorough pat-down, then a thin hand curls around the tent flap and eases it back. "Lita?"

"Yeah. What do you got for me?"

The girl stoops her head to get through the flap, then stands erect, hands at her sides. "Carlos Alvarez."

"Uh-huh. You and everybody else."

The girl shakes her head, her long hair swishing around. "I just saw him last night."

"Sure you did. Prove it." I give her my best dead-eyed stare and a slow, snakelike blink. "Dazzle me."

The girl's voice is breathier now, higher. "He was up in Lynnwood. At a camp in Scriber Lake Park."

Lynnwood? I don't even know where that is, but I'm not going to admit that to this girl. It's not in the city, I know that much, and Rosie would never leave the city. This girl is lying. Another dead end.

My hands tighten around the knife's hilt and I grimace against a sudden sharp headache. I want to fling my knife at this pissant, but I don't have the energy to clean up the blood after. "I don't believe you. Get out."

"No, it's true. He showed up there last night with some shrimpy girl, asked to borrow a car."

I bolt upright in my chair. "He was with a girl?"

My visitor must see the spark of excitement in my eyes because she edges forward from the tent flap. "Yeah," she says, licking her lips. "A real runt. Came up to here on me." She holds her hand flat, just below her chin.

"What did she look like?" I ask.

The girl shrugs. "Brown hair, light brown eyes. Thin. She's got a scar under her right eye." The girl smiles evilly.

I feel my eyes harden. "I don't recall a scar."

The girl wipes the smile off her face and straightens her shoulders. "It's new."

I clear my throat and narrow my eyes. "What was her name?" I snap.

A wrinkle appears between the girl's eyebrows. "Name? I

don't even know if she has one. Carlos called her 'Boo.'" Her lips twist with distaste.

Boo. Of course he does. How sickeningly sweet. It's them.

I relax back into my chair, my mind already elsewhere, planning. Lynnwood. Scriber Lake Park. What on Earth is she doing there? I glance at the girl, who stands uncertainly in the middle of my tent. "You pass," I tell her. "Your information is accurate, and I'll make sure you're properly rewarded. What's your name?"

The girl tilts her head and gives me a smile that borders on flirtatious. "Angel."

"Thank you, Angel."

The girl nods. "Um…"

"Yes?"

"That shrimpy chick with Carlos…I want her gone. Out of the picture. Can you do that?"

I lean forward, my hands laced together, swinging between my knees. I feel my eyes glitter like a thousand chips of glass. "That's exactly my plan."

The visitor has just ducked out of the tent when I'm wracked by convulsions. My arms and legs spasm and twitch erratically. I stare at my limbs with horror. I can't stop the jolting movements. Have I been poisoned? Did Angel hit me with some kind of dart? What's happening?

I lose all track of time, giving myself over completely to the seizure. When I come to, I've bitten my tongue and my mouth is full of blood.

I look down at my clothing. The seams on my camo pants are split in the thighs. My T-shirt stretches painfully tight across my breasts, which suddenly seem enormous. I wrap my arms protectively across my chest. They don't feel like my arms anymore. They're longer and even stronger than before. I stretch my hand out in front of me and spread my fingers. My bones have no hint of their old twist. My digits are as straight as an arrow. As straight as the arrow I almost shot through Rosie's heart days ago.

Rosie. I close my eyes as a memory assails me. We're sitting across from each other on a meal break during training. Rosie's giving me all her legs because she knows they're my favorite. Rosie says she prefers the body, but she doesn't mean it. The body is bland and mealy. The legs are where all the flavor is.

I accept Rosie's gift and stuff a handful in my mouth, savoring the slightly salty flavor and the crunch. "Mmm." I sigh with satisfaction. Rosie smiles and wipes at the corner of her own mouth. I giggle and feel my face. A leg dangles out of the corner of my mouth, and I tuck it in, licking my lips and smiling at Rosie, my letter-mate, my life partner, my best friend.

What is that I'm eating? What is it called?

They're spiders, of course, my brain supplies almost automatically. *You've been eating them your whole life.* And yet…I haven't. I can't explain it any better than that, but I *feel* like this is new. No, I don't just feel like it, I *know* it's new, though my brain is arguing and supplying all sorts of supporting evidence to back itself up.

I've been eating them once a month since I was born. Sometimes, in a banner year, twice a month. They're delicious. There's no other food in the towers so satisfying. The legs. My mouth waters just thinking about them.

I drag the back of my hand across my face, wiping the drops of saliva that have burst from my tongue.

I shake my head, then smack myself across the face. One of the thin new scars on my face splits and seeps a trickle of blood. Am I cracking? Has the stress of losing Rosie finally gotten to me?

No. I grit my teeth and picture the girl who just left my tent, the one with the vital information. I haven't lost Rosie. I just misplaced her in Lynnwood.

I dig in my back pocket and pull out the smartphone I stole earlier, then I google Scriber Lake Park. I stand up and the top of my head presses against the inside of the tent's roof. It's never done that before.

I look at my clothes again, my T-shirt stretched tight and threadbare, my pants in tatters, seams ripped and torn. My toes hang an inch over the edge of my flip-flops. I've grown, rapidly and unexplainably.

I frown at the smartphone. It's too late to catch a bus to Lynnwood, but that's fine. I can swipe a wallet or two and take a cab. I need new clothes first. And could I even find the encampment in the pitch darkness? What if I wandered lost in the woods all night?

I grit my teeth. This sucks. I glare at the smartphone again. It's just after one in the morning. I'll dig up some clothes here in The Jungle, pick a pocket or two on the streets, and take a cab north. By the time I get there, day should be breaking. I'm not wasting time. I'm being smart. I see quick movement out of the corner of my eye, and it's like fate is sending me a message. I shoot my hand out, pinch the creature between my fingers, and stuff it in my mouth. Delicious.

CHAPTER THREE

July 7, 2018 – Rosie

I can't sleep. Carlos takes deep, even breaths beside me. I wriggled out of his arms an hour ago. I wish I hadn't. If my brain was going to keep me up, firing one panicked thought after another through my frontal cortex, I'd rather suffer through it in the safety of his embrace. But I don't want to wake him up, so I sit on the tent floor beside him, my knees pulled up to my chest.

I haven't had any more seizures because I haven't been assailed by any new memories. Is that because I haven't learned anything new that I take with me into the future that will change my society enough to affect me from the moment I'm born? That's what I assume.

But now that I know that I'm Rosarita Columbia, that I'm the one who prepares and saves humanity from extinction during The Collapse, shouldn't every single thing I do change the course of history?

No, I decide. Everything I do now creates the history that I already know. I don't think I'm going to have too many episodes of new knowledge changing everything. We have hydroponic floors. We have moth pollination. We have time travel. We have all those things and many more that I already know about. So spiders as protein is new. And I'm glad for it. I grew several inches just now. I'm sure the rest of my people did too. Most of them just didn't suffer through the spasms and pain that I did because they're not time travelers. They don't have dual time-lines. I have memories of another timeline that they do not, a timeline that doesn't exist anywhere outside my own thoughts. Just one.

Did Dad and General Safeco experience inexplicable wracking pain and a sudden growth spurt just now? They're both time travelers and they're both involved with my travel, though in different ways. So they'd have access to the dual timeline memories, wouldn't they? It's also possible that neither man noticed the difference and wouldn't even recognize the dual timelines without a thorough search of their own memories. Safeco was a teenager during The Collapse, so he was probably already mostly grown. The inclusion of spiders in a post-Collapse diet wouldn't have affected him much. Grandmother took excellent care of Dad and made sure he had the best nutrition so he would grow into a strong capable person who could lead The Towers after she was gone, so the inclusion of spiders might have helped, but he was already tall and strong to begin with.

I interrupt my own train of thought. No, my grandmother didn't do that. *I did that*. I raised David Columbia. I took care of him. I brought him up to be a powerful leader. I'm sixteen years old! How will I know the first thing about taking care of a baby?

I'm so glad right now that Dad told me he was adopted before I got trapped in this time, or 'meltdown' wouldn't begin to describe what I'd be feeling. The Collapse is nine and a half months from now. That means Dad doesn't exist at all right now.

Not even as like, a zygote. Who is his mother? How do I end up with him?

I close my eyes and picture my dad with his stern, stoic expression that he wears ninety-nine percent of the time as he faces the problems of The Towers head on, and then I try to picture him as a baby, a squalling infant. I can't do it. Then I think of Dad's 'every once in a while' expression. When his countenance melts into a warm crinkly face of love directed at me. Dad has to be hard, for The Towers. But for me, he's my daddy. And I'm so lucky.

I don't know how I'm going to learn to be a parent in the few months I have left to prepare. I also don't know how I'm going to Gila-shield large blocks of floors in The Towers to protect against radiation, or how I'm going to start spider and moth colonies, or install decon units on the roofs, or stockpile thousands of weapons and tens of thousands of rounds of ammunition, or how I'm going to learn to set up a whole system of hydroponic farming, or where I'm going to get the money for any of that.

I'd grown up believing I was a rich environmentalist that everyone thought was crazy. I'm not rich and I don't know the first thing about this environment. Plants? The only plants I know are the ones that grow on our hydroponic floors, which were already set up and fully functional the day I was born.

"Boo?" Carlos's groggy voice breaks into my increasingly panicky thoughts.

"Over here," I croak.

I watch his dark form struggle out of the blankets. At over six feet tall, he can't come close to standing in this tent, so he hunches over and moves to where I sit with my knees to my chest. His face is blurry and indistinct in the darkness, but his warmth is familiar and comforting when he puts his arm around me.

I tilt my head back and he kisses me just above my left

eyebrow. "You okay?" he asks. "Your breathing woke me up. It sounded like you were hyperventilating or something. You didn't have another...thing...did you?"

"No, I didn't get any new memories. I'm just sitting here trying to figure out how to grow enough dandelions and milk thistle to feed ten thousand people. No biggie."

"Why do you grow weeds instead of real vegetables?"

"I don't know! Because that's what we grow. I didn't pick it."

But as soon as the words are out of my mouth, I question myself. If I didn't pick our crops, then who did? "I don't know why anything is the way it is," I say quietly, my flash of sarcastic anger gone now. "I don't know how to do any of this."

Carlos falls silent for so long, I don't think he's going to respond to me, so when he does, I'm surprised. And I'm doubly surprised by the words that come out of his mouth.

"I think I can help you with the hydroponics."

CHAPTER FOUR

July 7, 2018 – Ellen

I scratch my neck, silently but vigorously, and check under my fingernails. Ugh. How many mosquitoes has that been now? Two dozen? I picked the wrong tree as home base for my stakeout.

But it's too late to change locations now. The sun rose hours ago, and still there's no movement in the camp below me. But this has to be the place.

I took a cab to Scriber Lake Park, arriving just before daybreak, and with Angel's insider information, it wasn't difficult to follow the subtle signs to the homeless camp. Rosie will crawl out of one of these tents any minute. She'll have morning business to take care of, and that's when I'll extract her – whether she wants to be recovered or not. I've planned for both contingencies.

But I'm not going to ruin it all with a stupid, selfish move. I'm not going to climb down from this tree to find a less buggy one and miss my chance to snag Rosie before Carlos Velcros himself to her side again.

Below, a wet chesty cough breaks the silence, and I tense in the crook of the tree branch, my muscles coiled and ready, full of nervous energy.

That seems to be the wake-up call the rest of the camp has been waiting for because all around the ring of tents, noises filter up. Yawns, groans, the rustling sounds of blankets being thrown back and sleeping bags being struggled out of. I recognize these sounds; I know this world. It's not that different from what I grew up with in The Towers, though these people have far more privacy than I did, and a much better diet.

A pale arm snakes around a tent flap. Carlos? No, Carlos's skin is darker than that. It doesn't mean they didn't share their tent with a third person. The arm turns out to belong to a redheaded man with sparse, patchy facial hair. Definitely not Carlos. The young man stretches and yawns, revealing stumpy discolored teeth. I narrow my eyes. The redhead reminds me of a slightly older version of Boris, a guy from my time. Boris has no letter-mate and I always watch my back around him because I know he gleefully anticipates my death and wouldn't mind giving me a nudge in that direction if he thought he could get away with it. I instantly hate the guy in the clearing below me. He looks so much like Boris that he could be his dad. I shake my head. *Don't be stupid. Of course he can't.* This guy is a zed; he's dead in less than a year.

He stretches, his too-small T-shirt riding up to reveal a pale, hairy belly, which he scratches languidly. *Gross.* He hocks and retches, clearing his throat in an exaggerated fashion, then spits a thick glob into the bushes next to my tree. No one else crawls out of his tent, and I'm finding myself glad that Rosie wasn't forced to bunk with that guy. Not that I'm rooting for Carlos.

Another tent shows activity now, and two young women crawl out of the flap. One heads directly down the girls' privacy path. The other reaches into a cooler and pulls out a can of some liquid, which she pops open and guzzles, a droplet oozing out of the corner of her mouth.

I swallow involuntarily. My throat is dry, lumpy, and jealous.

Now there's lots of activity in the rest of the ring of tents and my eyes dart back and forth from flap to flap as I catalog all the people who are not Rosie and Carlos.

One tent remains undisturbed and quiet. That must be theirs. Almost as soon as I think the thought, the girl who just slaked her thirst crosses to the silent dome.

She taps her finger against the sidewall of the tent, making the whole frame quiver. "Carlos? Rosie? You all right in there?"

I shiver with anticipation and wait for the response.

And wait.

And wait.

Something drips on me from above, hitting me in the head and rolling down my left cheek, but I don't move. I'm frozen like a gargoyle. The girl on the ground seems disturbed as well because she really rattles the tent this time when she slaps her hand against the side. "You guys? You okay? I'm coming in."

I tremble with anticipation as she throws back the flap, drops to all fours, and crawls inside.

Barely an instant later, she's crawling back out with a piece of paper in her hand, her expression completely unperturbed, which is the exact opposite of how I feel. Her eyes scan the paper, back and forth, back and forth. She kneels, rocks back on her heels, and reads quietly for at least thirty seconds, then flips it over and scans the back side of the page.

One of the men in the clearing asks the question I'm dying to get the answer to. "They okay?"

The girl pushes herself to standing and brushes the piece of paper against her leg. "I guess so."

She guesses so? What is that supposed to mean? A whole page full of scribbled information and 'she guesses so'?

The man adjusts his thick-rimmed eyeglasses and rubs the back of his neck. "Freaked me out when she had that seizure."

Rosie had a seizure? I remember my own experience last night and it's so real that for a moment, I forget where I am. I sway in the tree limbs high above the campground and just manage to dig my fingertips into bark before I slip off my branch.

"Yeah, me too. Carlos says she's fine, though." Down below, the girl with the paper in her hand walks across the clearing and digs two cans out of the cooler. She offers one to the man with the glasses and they both snap their tabs open and drink. The girl wipes the back of her hand across her mouth and flutters the paper like it's not the most important thing in the whole entire world. "Carlos says not to worry. They took off early. Had some business to take care of."

Up in the tree branches, I bite the back of my hand to keep from crying out. They're gone? How many minutes did I miss them by? Did I pass them in the woods? And what kind of business could they possibly have to attend to? *Where are they?* I need to see that note.

The girl folds the paper up and tucks it in her back pocket. "You want me to make some coffee? I got instant."

"Sure," the guy replies. "I'll get a fire going."

"Not too big," the girl cautions. "We don't need to send a smoke signal in the daytime."

Grunting, the guy nods and other people wander around the campsite while my mind reels. Rosie is gone. Carlos took her away before daylight. Did he know I was coming? How? My heart lurches. Angel could have had second thoughts and warned him. I shake my head, trying to brush the thought from my mind. No way. I read zeds easily and Angel didn't flip. Not that quick. Angel wanted Rosie out of the picture, and she didn't care how.

Did Angel come back up here and take matters into her own

hands? Unlikely. If Angel were up here slinking around, there'd be no note. I've got to read that note.

The guy below in the clearing flicks a lighter and touches it to the base of a pile of wood. He puts his face right up to it, blows, then curses. "I suck at this."

The girl who offered him coffee clicks her tongue and joins him. "You can't just light the wood on fire directly. You gotta use kindling." She scrapes a few wood chips into a pile and tries the lighter, but it doesn't catch.

A bubble of dread climbs up my throat. I know exactly what's going to happen next and I start frantically climbing down, but by the time I leap from the last branch, howling, "No! Stop!" the crumpled-up note is already out of the girl's pocket and merrily ablaze.

CHAPTER FIVE

July 7, 2018 – Carlos

Rosie is as nervous as a cat. Not that she knows what one is.

I squeeze her hand, and she tries to smile at me, but not only does it fail to reach her eyes, it fails to reach her lips. They just flatten out in a slightly warbly line and she looks mildly queasy. If she's motion sick already, I can only imagine what it's going to be like when we load onto the ferry. The boat's not even here yet.

Rosie and I left the campsite before dawn. I still kind of regret blurting out that I could help teach her about indoor farming. Because the guy I know isn't raising radishes and rutabagas. He's one of Dad's old drug connections. I haven't seen any of these people since Dad got busted. And I haven't wanted to. But Rosie needs this information, and it's something I can provide for her. I get the feeling that there's not much that's going to keep her sane, and sitting in the middle of the woods in Lynnwood with a bunch of street kids is not what the doctor ordered right now.

So I opened my mouth and almost instantly regretted it.

Eddie Fitzgerald – Fast Eddie – my dad's old business partner, certainly knew a lot about how to grow plants indoors. He was also an expert in a lot of other aspects of the business, like evading the authorities and laundering money, and I really didn't want anything to do with him.

I chew my lip. I'm just as nervous as Rosie, but for very different reasons.

"Now boarding, Seattle to Bremerton. Seattle to Bremerton, now boarding." Crap. The boat pulled in behind us and I didn't even notice it.

I squeeze Rosie's hand one more time and help her to her feet. She takes a deep breath and turns around. "Where is it?" she asks.

I cock my head and point straight in front of us. "That's it, right there. The big green-and-white thing."

"That's the boat?" she says, astonishment in her voice. "I thought boats were small, like I don't know, fifty feet long or less."

"You've never noticed the ferry before?"

She shakes her head.

"Do you feel any better about getting on it now that you know how big it is?"

She shakes her head. "Not significantly."

I put my arm around her shoulders and squeeze her to my side. "Ferries are totally safe. Nothing bad can happen to you on this boat."

"You promise?"

I nod. "I do."

She takes a shaky breath. "Let's do this, then."

I know this is so far outside her comfort zone, it might as well be in a different comfort country, and I feel a surge of pride that she trusts me enough to do it anyway.

We walk through the terminal and across the little metal bridge that links the building to the ferry boat.

The ramp clangs as we walk across it, which I think will startle her, but it doesn't seem to bug her at all.

"Don't worry. That's just the metal bending," I assure her anyway.

"That doesn't bother me. It kind of reminds me of home."

"Let's walk around a little. Maybe you'll end up wanting to score one of these for your time."

Rosie purses her lips and I know I've said the right thing because suddenly her nerves are gone and she's all business. "Let's check it out."

We walk the ship from stem to stern. The boat shudders and pulls away from the dock out into open water, and the automated message begins, welcoming us to the Washington State Ferry service, and reminding us not to walk away from our bags. Like I would ever forget that. Everything I own is in my backpack.

"Where did all of these people come from?" Rosie asks. "They weren't all in the terminal with us."

"They've come up from their cars."

"There's cars on here?" Rosie grabs the railing. "Won't that make us sink?"

"Nah, we're okay. The cars are down below. They drive on, the people park, and a lot of them come up here to get food or go out on the deck or whatever."

"Can we go see?"

"The cars?"

She nods.

"Sure."

I lead her to a stairwell and we push the heavy metal door open, shoving it into the wind. Rosie's hair swirls around her face, long strands of it whipping across her eyes. She tips her head back and for a moment, with her chiseled, dark eyebrows and long eyelashes, she looks like a model for a line of gritty urban clothing. She's sexy as hell and I can't help myself, I tug her back to me and slide my hands down to her bottom while I kiss her thoroughly.

She returns my kisses with abandon and I think we both forget where we are for a minute, just a couple of kids on an adventure, fighting the wind.

"Excuse me," someone says in an amused tone, and I break away from Rosie so that a couple of women can walk upstairs past us. I'm sure I have a goofy grin on my face, and I touch my forehead to Rosie's. "You and me, Boo." I hope she gets what I mean by that, because I mean everything. Her and me against the world. Nothing's going to come between us – not Angel, not Fast Eddie, not The Collapse.

Her eyes shine up at me, and I think she knows.

We lace our fingers together and walk the rest of the way down the stairs side by side.

When we get to the car deck, the wind is intense, but not nearly as intense as the expression on Rosie's face. Her eyes dart around, taking in everything. We weave through the cars, Rosie in the lead, checking everything out. Finally, she looks at me and shakes her head. "No."

"No?"

She nods. "I can see why this won't work, why we don't have them in my time."

"Why not?"

"They're top-heavy. Any sort of violent waves kick up, this thing will go belly-up."

"There's violent waves all the time. Ferries are out in wind-storms; they almost never stop."

"Not the kind of storms we have in my time. The flooding caused dozens of nuclear reactors to melt down at the same time. The Earth fought back and it's still throwing punches. The climate is broken."

I fall silent at that. Somewhere well behind us on the auto deck, someone's car alarm goes off briefly. The insistent buzzing doesn't seem to bother Rosie at all, which surprises me. "You realize you've been on a boat now, out on the open water, for twenty minutes, and you're fine?" I say.

Rosie jerks back. A puzzled look flashes across her face, followed quickly by a thoughtful one. "You're right. I am fine. I haven't been freaked out since we left the dock."

"I think I know why. It's because you've been busy. You've been in planning mode. You're thinking about how you're going to save people, not how we're all going to die."

The ferry shudders as the captain shifts gears, and it doesn't faze her one bit. "You're right," she says. "When I'm thinking about strategy, I don't have any brain space, or even any desire, to be scared."

"Let's work with that." I squeeze her hand.

She shakes her head. "I don't know if I can be in crisis planning mode one hundred percent of the time. I know I should be. But I don't know if I can sustain it."

"No, crisis mode one hundred percent of the time is not what I'm suggesting. Because some of the time we should be doing this." I put my hands on her waist and tug her to me and our mouths meet. We kiss for several long moments as the wind whips around us and waves buffet the sides of the vessel. Salty spray fills the car deck, but my lungs are full of the scent of Rosie's skin and hair. I twist my fingers in her dark brown locks and marvel at how thick and shiny it is. I cup her chin and give her a last lingering kiss. "What do you say, like maybe forty percent crisis mode and sixty percent that? We'd have to take breaks for sleeping."

Rosie smiles at me with her eyes closed, and my heart swells. She doesn't smile for just anyone, let alone with closed eyes. I remember her joy when I showed her Lake Union on the Fourth of July, how she opened up her eyes and gasped at the beauty. If she thought the lake was special, Puget Sound will blow her away. And I think she's ready for it.

"Come on. Let's go up top," I say. "Now that you're not scared anymore, I want you to see the view from the deck. Wait until you see the Olympic Mountains from out here."

We go back up the stairs, then take another flight to the outside top deck. I push open the heavy door and Rosie walks through it, her hair whipping in the wind. I could watch that forever. She looks so wild and untamed.

Seagulls race the boat, and she stares at them, a look of wonder on her face. "God, I wish we still had birds. Just imagine the hope they could inspire."

"Maybe you can save a couple."

She squeezes her eyes shut tightly and cocks her head, then opens her eyes and shrugs. "I don't think so. If I were able to do that, wouldn't I have had a seizure just now?"

"Only if you farmed them and ate them."

A bubble of laughter escapes her lips and she claps her hand over her mouth. "Carlos!"

"What?" I ask playfully.

"None of this is supposed to be funny." She shakes her finger at me, but her eyes continue to sparkle.

I take her hand and give her lips a quick kiss. We stroll along the upper deck toward one of the pickleforks that jut out over the car deck. She scuffs her heel against the metal surface. "Seizure or not, I don't think I manage to figure out a way to save the birds." She raises her voice above the thrumming of the wind. "I thought about wanting to save them, but I don't have any new memories of birds now."

"Maybe it doesn't always work that way. Maybe today wasn't the day you figured out how to do it. Or maybe for little things, you don't get a flood of new memories. Maybe it's subtle enough that they're just in there now, and it doesn't have to be a major production."

Rosie gets a cute little wrinkle above her nose as she thinks, but there's something lurking behind her shining brown eyes. I don't know if it's sadness or fear, but something's really troubling her, I can tell.

She turns around and grips the rail, facing the water and letting the wind blast her. I do the same, standing by her side, and the wind makes my eyes water and forces tears from them. I glance sideways at Rosie and see that it's happening to her too.

"Want to go back inside?" I ask, lifting my voice above the wind.

"No," she says, the wind making her sound a little choked up.

I move to stand behind her, and I wrap my arms around her waist, holding her like the guy did with his girl in *Titanic*, feeling about as awesome as he must have. But in my version of this story, I will not sink below the water. Rosie is not going to have to make her way in the world without me.

I am not going down with the ship.

CHAPTER SIX

July 7, 2018 – Rosie

The dread is here, stronger than ever, as I stand at the railing with Carlos's arms around me and the wind in my face. Tears stream out of my eyes unbidden and I tremble, hoping he won't feel my shudders over the tremors of the powerful boat. In all the histories, all the stories, all the lore about my grandmother, Rosarita Columbia, the woman I now know is me – there is no mention of the man she loves.

In my time, we talk about how Rosarita saved us all, and I feel the awesome weight of that responsibility heavy on my shoulders. We talk about how Rosarita Columbia raised her son, David, to lead. Only I know that he's adopted. She – no, I – will rescue him on the day of The Collapse and raise him as my own. But what about Carlos? Where is he in our histories and legends?

It's amazing how quickly my fears wash away when I'm focused on strategy and preparation. It's like someone completely different takes over for me. I appreciate her, this person who takes charge of my emotions and banishes my phobias, but I'm also alarmed by her. I don't know where she puts the *me* that's *me* when she takes control.

It's not like a have a split personality. I really don't think that. It's just that all my terror and dread and scary thoughts find someplace to hide when I'm focused on disaster response mode, but I don't know where that hiding place is. And I kind of need to know. Now.

Because I have to figure out how to save Carlos. If I could solve that problem, all my other worries and fears will go away. The sick feeling of dread that lives twenty-four seven in the pit of my stomach could finally take a rest.

In 2074, we talk about how Rosarita taught us all to live sparingly, to conserve, to manage our bodies and our lifestyles for the new conditions. She taught us how to pack our lungs with stored oxygen, and how to avoid and escape radiation. She told us what skills to focus on, like climbing and breath control, to keep us alive and a half step ahead of danger.

We talk about all these things and more, but I've searched my memories a thousand times, probing my neural pathways incessantly, my eyes wide open, while I should be sleeping soundly in Carlos's arms.

And he's not there.

No one talks about how Rosarita did it all with the love of her life by her side. I have no memories of the legend of Carlos. Carlos doesn't exist in our lore, and that can only mean one thing.

Carlos is going to leave me.

Every time we talk about our feelings for each other, or our plans for the future, I squeeze my eyes shut tightly and breathe deeply through my nose, almost to the point of hyperventilating, waiting desperately, longingly for the headache. I search for the new memories. The legacy stories that I've grown up with, detailing the love and resilience of Carlos and Rosarita, the duo who faced The Collapse head on and beat the odds – together.

Those memories never come. Every stabbing headache leaves me with something new, but it's never Carlos. And somewhere inside, I know that it never will be. Carlos will abandon me. Maybe not today, maybe not tomorrow, but somehow, I will screw this up. I just don't know when.

But it happens. It must.

I shudder hard, and Carlos's arms tighten around me. Tears pour out of my eyes, blown back by the wind.

Why does he leave me? How do I ruin this? Why would he choose death in The Collapse instead of life with me? What could I possibly do that is so horrible? And how can I stop myself?

Carlos kisses my neck, and I reach back to stroke his cheek. I lift my face to the sun, wondering how many more kisses I have left, knowing that every single one he gives me might be my last.

CHAPTER SEVEN

July 7, 2018 – Ellen

"**W**hat did it say?" I scream.

The group in the clearing looks at me, dumbfounded.

"The note," I demand. "What did it say? Tell me." I narrow my eyes to slits and use my most commanding voice. "Now."

The young woman who appears to be the leader of this place bristles at my tone, and she stands up from where she's been crouched by the fire. Her eyes harden and she folds her arms across her chest in the universal symbol of 'make me.'

Oh, I could make her, all right. My eyes dart around the clearing, cataloging enemy positions and sketching rapid plans. I could kill four of these people before I'd have to switch to 'wound and incapacitate' mode. Most of these people would probably flee at the first death, though, especially if I took out their leader. But I can't. She's the one who read the note. I need her alive.

Damn it. I have to play this situation completely differently, and I'm already off on the wrong foot. I'm not going to get what I want by fighting. I have to be nice. *Frack.* Of all my survival skills, that's the one I'm worst at.

I hold my hands out at my sides and belatedly try to slap a pleading look on my face. It shouldn't be that hard to get the expression right since I desperately need information from the girl standing in front of me, but I'm not used to kowtowing to zeds, so I don't know how successful I am at looking subservient.

"I'm sorry." My voice is sickeningly sweet. "I didn't mean to startle you. I've just been looking for my litt—" I stop myself from saying 'litter-mate' by pretending to choke back a sob. "Little cousin," I blurt after a moment's hesitation.

"In the trees?" the girl with the crossed arms says sarcastically.

"I was sleeping up there. I didn't want you to freak out if you found me in your campsite unexpectedly." I shrug. "I heard she was staying at an encampment in this park, so I climbed a tree and decided to watch so I could figure out if she was here without disturbing you."

The guy who was trying to light the fire murmurs something in the girl's ear. I have sharp hearing, so I catch what he says, though I keep my face impassive.

"That's Lita," he whispers in her ear, "Jimmy Squint's girl."

I have to restrain myself from rolling my eyes. Why is it always 'so and so's girl' with these people? Jimmy is my puppet. Don't these zeds know anything?

The girl's eyes widen at his words and I feel a smug little sense of satisfaction. My reputation preceded me, and I have to admit I feel a bit proud about it. Unfortunately, my reputation is not going to help me here because the girl's eyes harden and her voice is a snarl. "Your cousin? I don't know what you're talking about." She spits on the ground. "That note was from a guy I know. You're barking up – and sleeping in – the wrong tree."

"I know it was from a guy." I glare at her on instinct but immediately soften my expression. "I know who wrote it. Carlos. Rosie's staying with Carlos."

The girl's jaw twitches just enough to tell me she's starting to bend a little, so I continue and I latch on to something utterly brilliant. "Rosie has seizures. And I have her medicine." I pat my pocket. "She could die without it."

"I knew it." The girl gasps, and her whole countenance changes. "She tried to play it off as no big deal, but she's lowkey that way, I can tell. Shit." She cocks her head at me. "Are you really Lita? Jimmy Squint's Lita?"

I grit my teeth. "Yes."

The girl's eyes glint in a way that tell me they're just about to harden again.

"What's your name?" I ask quickly. That's what people are supposed to do when they're being friendly. And I've got to convince this girl that I'm not a threat.

"Jordan." She takes a step back and shoves her fists in her front pockets. The waistband of her shorts dips down, giving me a peekaboo view of her navel.

It's hard to tear my eyes away from her flat belly, but I force myself to, and I muster up every bit of charm I have in my body. "Jordan, thank you for giving shelter to my cousin. I love her so much, and I miss her. Yes, I am Lita, and I'm sure you've heard some stuff about me. Some of it's true. Some of it's not." I swallow and clasp my hands together in front of my heart. "But I love my little cousin and I'll do anything to find her and make sure she's okay. Please, please, help me and you'll have my undying gratitude. I will owe you a favor, one that I could potentially never repay, though I would try. Anything you need, I will give you. Just please help me find Rosie."

Did I lay it on too thick? Frack. Probably. Jordan is quiet way too long. Everyone in this stupid clearing is as silent as a stone. Jordan's control over these people seems absolute. She's a natural leader. Suddenly, I realize I don't just want information from her. I want to win her over. I want her on my side.

"Dammit. I knew she was sick," Jordan says, stamping one foot. "She said she was fine, but it didn't sit right with me. I knew I should have kept a closer eye on her."

"You helped her, which is more than most strangers would do, and I'm grateful. I have her medicine and I've been trying to get it to her, but you know…the streets…" I trail off and allow a haunted note into my voice. "I haven't been able to catch up with her," I finish. "I always show up one day too late." I kick a rock. "And it happened again."

Jordan takes a step toward me, away from the fire, which has sputtered out. "They shouldn't be gone long. Carlos says he's planning to come back for a job," she says softly.

For a split second, I try to control my emotions, but then I remember that she'll expect me to be jubilant, so I let the joy flood over me.

"They're coming back! When? Did they say where they went?"

Jordan shakes her head, and I can tell she's warming up, but she's still wary of me, and I respect that. "He said that they'd be gone a couple days taking care of some business. Nothing specific."

I'm not sure if I believe her, but I have no other choice. The stupid note is burnt to ashes.

I lock eyes with Jordan. Her lips part slightly, she relaxes her tightly folded arms, and I know that I'm in. "Can I stay here and wait for them to come back?" I ask.

"If I say *no*, will you stay here anyway?"

This girl can spot a liar, I'm sure of it, so I nod solemnly. "Yes, but you'd never notice. I'd stay out of sight and not bother you at all."

Jordan bobs her head curtly, seeming to appreciate my honesty, and her words back up that assessment. "All right. You can stay." Her voice grows extra sharp. "But we have rules here. This is not a place for junkies or burnouts. We don't allow kids, but we're a young camp, teens and early twenties only. Anyone who can remember anything about the nineties isn't welcome here. No needles in my camp and I have a zero-tolerance policy for meth. Whatever else you want to alter your mind or body with is your business. There's absolutely no panhandling in the park, and we respect each other here. Consent matters, no means no, etcetera."

"Perfect."

"Welcome to Scriber Lake, Lita."

I decide to take one more risk. I'm not sure why, but it feels right, so I go for it. I close the last couple of feet between us. "Lita is my street name, and I don't feel like I need to be that person here. Rosie doesn't even know me as Lita." I put my callused palm on Jordan's upper arm in a gentle, non-threatening way. "Please. Call me Ellen."

CHAPTER EIGHT

July 7, 2018 – Carlos

"*Now arriving Bremerton. This is Bremerton.*"

A pleasant tone bing-bongs and walk-on passengers, like us, begin to queue up on the pickleforks. The captain lines the boat up between thick wooden logs standing upright, belted together with metal cord. They thrust up out of the water and serve as bumpers. The boat coasts on forward momentum and nudges gently against the dock. We drift sideways to the left and knock up against one of the wooden guides. Below, ferry workers toss ropes to each other and lash the boat to the dock, winding the rope over and under thick metal spurs on either side of the front of the car deck.

"Simple but effective," Rosie says, nodding approval. "That's how we secure our tower canoes when we don't bring them inside."

"Maybe one of your fifty thousand Collapse survivors was a Washington State Ferry employee."

"Maybe," Rosie says. "Or maybe we just got lucky with a cordage and knots enthusiast."

A worker on the ferry terminal side lowers a retractable passenger bridge while a worker on this side secures it to the deck, and we walk off. On the way, Rosie gives the ferry worker an up and down look, as if she's memorizing his features.

"Gonna keep an eye out for him when you're sitting on the admittance panel?" I ask, only slightly sarcastically.

Rosie rolls her eyes but lifts her shoulder slightly. "Maybe," she says, and from the tone of her voice, I think she might be serious.

We walk through the terminal and out onto the street. "Man, this place has changed a lot," I say absentmindedly.

"Not as much as it's going to change next year."

I grit my teeth involuntarily. As much as I adore this girl, I'm kind of getting tired of her constant negativity and reminders about how everything gets destroyed in April. "Yeah, I get it," I say. "It was just an observation."

"I'm not trying to be a jerk," Rosie says, dropping my hand. "It's just reality."

I stuff my hands in my pockets and cross the street. "Too bad you didn't visit Bremerton in 2006 or something on one of your trips to the past. Then we could have a conversation instead of you just immediately talking about how it's all going to be wiped out and everyone's gonna die."

"Carlos, I'm sorry," Rosie says in a tiny voice. "This is really hard for me."

I take her hand back into mine and pull her past the dive bars that line the waterfront street. "I know you're less anxious when you're in survival planning mode," I say, trying to keep my voice gentle, "but try not to shoot everything I say down, okay?"

She nods, unusually acquiescent. "I'm sorry," she says again.

I hug her to my side and kiss the top of her head. "I'm sorry too. I guess if I'm being honest, I'm kind of in the mood to pick a fight."

"What's going on, Carlos?"

I shake my head and lead Rosie around the corner. From here we'll walk slightly uphill until we get to Burwell, the main road that will lead us to Fast Eddie's neighborhood. "I have huge reservations about you meeting this guy. I know you need to know all you can about indoor farming, but I feel like maybe I spoke too soon. Yeah, sure, I know a guy who can help you learn, but do I really want to make this introduction?" I answer my own question without pausing. "No. I don't."

"Why not?"

We've reached the corner of Burwell and Pacific, and I press the button and tap my foot nervously, waiting for the light to change. "My dad never would have gotten into the mess he's in if he hadn't met Eddie," I blurt out. "They were partners in the whole thing, and I have no idea how Eddie didn't end up going down when Dad did because Eddie's the actual criminal in the situation. He masterminded the whole thing, and he was into way more stuff than just growing pot. Illegal gambling, for one. I think he fenced guns. There was other stuff that I'm not sure about, but I have suspicions. Dad tried to keep me out of it, for my own good, but I saw more than he knew I did. I protected Ricky as much as I could, and he was just young enough to be mostly oblivious. Anyway, somehow Eddie stayed a step ahead of the police, and Dad didn't rat him out, that's for sure. But he's a sleazy dude, and now that we're on this side of the water, every cell in my body is telling me this is a terrible idea. We can figure out some other way. Any other way."

The light changes. Rosie glances left toward where the ferry sits at the dock, loading passengers for the return trip to Seattle, then she turns her eyes forward again and stoically crosses the street. I take a deep breath, let it out with a shudder, and follow her. Rosie is quiet for a long time as we walk the big up-and-down rolling hills of Burwell.

I match her strides, which are shorter than my own. I don't want to go this way, but I'm not leaving her alone. Finally, she speaks. "Do you know anyone else who knows anything about indoor farming and hydroponics? Where to purchase the equipment? Or how to install it?"

I grunt and feel my mouth quirking down. "Uh, no."

"I don't, either. And we simply don't have time for me to learn it at the library, Carlos. I need someone I can talk to, ask specific questions, get knowledgeable answers."

I nod. I get it. I hate it, but I get it.

"But I promise you," she goes on, "I'm a quick learner. I know more about this stuff already than the average person, even the average person from my time. I've inspected the hydroponic floors in my tower for the last two years. Dad trusts me. He started training me on it when I was fourteen."

A cop car races past us, heading downtown, lights blaring. I stop and flinch involuntarily at the gust of wind the zooming car pushes in our direction. Rosie turns to face me and takes both my hands in hers. "So I don't need much from this guy Eddie," she says. "Just very basic stuff. Where to buy the equipment. How to get it delivered where I need it. Maybe pointers on the initial install. Stuff he can tell me in one meeting, maybe two." She gets up on her tiptoes so her eyes are closer to mine. "I promise I'm not going to drag this out. You won't have to be around him for very long."

I nod, dip my head, and kiss her soft, parted lips. She sighs and her cheeks color prettily. I hug her tightly, then shade my eyes and look past her at a street sign. "We're only a couple blocks away, Boo. Left at the next cross street."

Rosie takes a quivering breath, chews on her bottom lip, then goes up on tiptoe to kiss me again. "Thank you," she whispers.

"Let's go get this over with," I say, my voice husky.

When we turn left on Fast Eddie's street, the Puget Sound spreads out before us again and Rosie gasps. I follow her gaze. We're facing the shipyard, the biggest industry in the whole area. You get so used to it when you live in its shadow that the gargantuan military vessels don't even faze you. It gets so you barely notice them, but I realize what the view would be like for someone who's never seen a bristling military base before.

"Forget ferries," Rosie breathes. "Why don't we have one of those?"

I stop, brace my hands on my knees, and laugh. "I imagine they're tough to steal."

Rosie points at an aircraft carrier. "That one over there could house a whole city."

"That's what they say," I agree. "I'm not sure which one that is. The Carl Vinson maybe? I don't know. Boats come and go all the time. But yeah, they say being on one is like being in a floating city. Thousands of people living on the same ship – so many you could be stationed there for years and not meet everyone."

"How is it powered?" Rosie asks.

"I don't know. Nuclear maybe? But seriously, I really don't know."

"I want one."

I cock my head and smile at her. "You're hoping for a headache, aren't you?"

"Frack yeah, I am. There's airplanes on the deck, do you see them? Do you know what I could do with those?"

She squeezes her eyes shut tightly, screws up her face, and, I assume, hopes really hard. Then she sighs, opens her eyes, and stares are her palms, turning them back and forth in front of herself. "Nope. Nothing. We don't get one."

"Doesn't hurt to try," I console, putting my arm around her shoulders and hugging her to my side. I feel like I've got my sweet Rosie back and I don't want to let her go. "I'll get you one someday. How about that?"

"You promise?" she asks, taking my hands, her eyes shining.

I'm feeling reckless, so I answer immediately. "Absolutely."

The shine in her eyes threatens to turn to tears, and I realize that I honestly mean what I just said. And who knows? After The

Collapse, maybe one of those warships would be mine for the taking. Feeling stronger and more powerful than I did a few seconds ago, I tug on her hands.

"Eddie lives at the end of this block, the green house on the left. C'mon."

CHAPTER NINE

July 7, 2018 – Rosie

Carlos knocks briskly on the door, *rap rap rap*. It's obvious from his mannerisms that he can't wait to get this over and done with, and I strengthen my resolve to be one hundred percent no-nonsense. I'm not going to wander off on weird tangents or try to squeeze anything else out of this person besides the basics.

And what I said to Carlos was true. I do know this stuff pretty well. But the systems I've inspected have already been up and operational. What I really don't understand – have no idea about, honestly – is where to get them. I've stolen thousands of syringes from needle exchanges, I've raided hospital storerooms for antibiotics and painkillers. I know how to get multivitamins, batteries, bandages, and ointments. But never in all my travels have I stumbled across hydroponic farming equipment. Is there, like, a general store for that? Or do you have to order it on the internet? If so, where on Earth do I have it shipped when I don't have an address? And of course, the big question – how do I get this all with no money? The unanswered logistical details slice at me like a thousand little paper cuts.

This person Carlos knows might be able to sweep much of that aside and cut to the chase of what I need. Someone does, right? Because all those hydroponic floors exist in 2074; I still remember them.

I close my eyes as Carlos hammers on the door again and I rifle through my memories, row after row of glass and steel growing racks, green plants dangling from each, growing under artificial lights without soil. Men and women in the cleanest lab coats in the towers, walking slowly up and down the aisles, misting precious clean water onto the growing plants. My memories are clear and solid.

My thoughts shift to Harvest Day when precious greens are gently cut free and prepared for distribution to the floors. Yes, it's all still there. I don't have any parallel memories of broken equipment or starving citizens. All I can visualize is hydroponic success.

Carlos bangs on the door some more. "This is weird," he says. "Eddie doesn't go anywhere. Or at least he didn't used to. People come to him. I used to think he was agoraphobic."

"What's that?"

"An irrational fear of being out in public or open spaces or something like that. After Dad got busted, I realized it wasn't a syndrome – it was just another way Eddie stayed ahead of the cops. He sat back and let other people take the risks." His jaw tightens. "He's obviously not planning on opening the door."

"We can't just go home," I say. "We came all this way. And we're running out of time."

Carlos expels an aggravated grunt, then balls his fist and pounds the front door. "Eddie!" he yells. "Open up."

He's about to pound again when someone wrenches the door inward. "Jesus, what is wrong with you?" A woman with puffy red hair and dark circles under her eyes stands at the threshold. She's wearing a negligee and a thin bathrobe.

Carlos and I both take an involuntary step back. "Oh," Carlos exclaims. "I'm sorry to...wake you. I'm looking for Eddie Fitzgerald."

She squints at us. First me, even though I'm the silent one, then at Carlos.

"He ain't here," she says, but there's something in her voice that tells me she's lying. No, not lying...just not entirely telling the truth.

"We just need to ask him a few questions," I say.

Carlos groans and turns to me, his eyes rolling so severely in his head that I can practically hear them clicking inside the sockets. "Could you sound any more like a cop?" he asks sarcastically, then turns back to the woman.

"Eddie's an old friend of my dad's. I'm not here looking for anything, not money, not, you know... anything. I was just hoping to see him for a few."

The woman squints again, then scrabbles in the pocket of her threadbare bathrobe and pulls out a pair of glasses. She puts them on, and her eyes seem to double in size. Now, instead of squinting, her eyelids pop wide open. "Losi?" she whispers.

Now it's Carlos's turn to squint and tilt his head. "Evelyn?"

"Oh my god." She gasps, then the next thing I know she's thrown her arms around Carlos and is dragging him through her front door. I shove my way in too, and I'm about to leap onto her back like a monkey when I realize after a split second that she's not attacking him, she's hugging him, and he's hugging her back.

She thrusts him away as if to get a better look at him and I bob out of the way so he doesn't stumble into me. Evelyn holds onto his shoulders, and she tips her head back to stare at his face. "Losi! What happened to my little friend? You're nine feet tall!"

Carlos laughs and blushes. "Evelyn used to babysit me," he says to me.

"He was the cutest little thing, him and his brother both. God, how long has it been? Eight years? No, that can't be right. How's Ricky?" Evelyn babbles, her words running together.

Carlos only answers her last question. "Doing great," Carlos says. "Straight A's. Total science nerd."

Evelyn's wide grin broadens. She has totally transformed from a suspicious sharp-faced redhead to a pretty woman about ten years older than me.

Seeming to notice herself for the first time, Evelyn gasps. "Oh!" she grabs the sides of her bathrobe and crisscrosses them around herself, covering up her lavender negligee. "I'm sorry. I was up late with the baby."

"You're a mom?" Carlos asks, surprise in his voice.

She nods proudly. "I am. Married too. She points over her shoulder at the shipyard. My husband's at work. Our little girl is nine months old."

"Congratulations, that's amazing," Carlos says warmly.

Evelyn smiles tightly. "I've come up."

"You always rose above," Carlos says, and I realize their conversation has gone off on a path that only they understand. I clear my throat, mostly to remind them that I'm still standing there.

"Oh!" Evelyn exclaims. She's a loud person, now that she's lost her suspicious tone. She talks in mostly exclamation points. "I'm being rude. Come in, come in."

We're already inside, so what does she want? For us to go deeper into her shadowy house? Carlos gives me a quick glance and I feel my lips tighten. My feelings must be written all over my face because Carlos's shoulders sag a little and his voice turns apologetic. "I wish we could, but I've really got to see Eddie. I have some business stuff I need to ask him."

"Losi..." Evelyn says in a warning tone.

"Don't worry," Carlos says. "It's completely legit. Totally aboveboard."

She cocks her head but doesn't say anything.

"Is Eddie here?" Carlos asks. "I figured he would be, but..." His voice trails off and he holds his hands at his sides. "I guess it's been a long time," he finishes.

"Eddie's my landlord now," Evelyn says. "He's got a new place. And a new name," she says, an odd note in her voice. "He goes by Edward these days."

Carlos pulls his head back in a double take. "Really?" he says, stretching the word out into three syllables.

Evelyn nods. "Really. He's very particular about it."

"Noted."

All three of us sort of shuffle around on our feet for a bit. Carlos and Evelyn obviously don't know how to continue the conversation, so I jump in before things turn totally awkward. "Can you give us his new address? We only need like an hour of his time. If that."

Evelyn recoils a bit, but she looks at Carlos, and he nods. "You promise no funny business?" she asks him.

"I swear," Carlos affirms.

She huffs a heavy sigh. "Give me a sec. I'll write down his address for you."

She disappears inside the house and from somewhere toward the back, I hear a baby's plaintive cry.

Evelyn is back in a flash, her baby's wails apparently spurring her to move quickly. She scribbles numbers and a street name on a scrap of paper and hands it to Carlos.

He looks at it and whistles. "Rocky Point?"

Evelyn nods and glances over her shoulder toward the sounds of the baby.

"How far away is it?" I ask Carlos.

"It'll take hours," he says glumly.

"You walked here? Of course you did," Evelyn says, answering her own question. She reaches in her pocket and draws out a key ring. "You drive?" she asks Carlos.

He nods.

"Borrow my car," Evelyn offers. "It'll help get you past the gate. Tell the guard who you are, obviously, and that you checked in with me first."

"The guard?" Carlos says incredulously.

Evelyn's eyes are shadowy. "Edward," she says, a biting tone in her voice, "has come up too."

CHAPTER TEN

July 7, 2018 – Ellen

Jordan runs a tight ship, and her firm leadership is undeniable. She has an impressive ability to bring directionless people together. Not even fifteen minutes after accepting me into their camp, everyone is eating, resources have been divvied up, jobs assigned, and schedules coordinated.

She'd be a great floor manager in a tower. In my world, I'm sure she'd be assigned to one of the premium buildings. Of course, realistically, if she were transplanted to my world, she'd probably die quickly. She'd fall down an open shaft and not be able to climb out, or she'd get swept away by a sneaker wave, something like that. She hasn't had a lifetime of learning to survive in my vertical world. But it's still a nice thing to imagine, Jordan in 2074, issuing orders, delegating tasks, quirking her sexy half-smile at me from behind hooded eyes when she thought I wasn't looking.

Wait, what did I just think? My cheeks grow hot. Is this a fever? Fevers are nonexistent in the towers, where everything is chilly and clammy. When you get sick your temperature is more likely to dive, but I had a fever once when I first came here a little more than a year ago. Some virus that I had no immunity to attacked me, but that feeling came on slowly, overnight, and this is different. This flush is accompanied by a not-unpleasant fluttering in my stomach and an increased heartrate.

Is this some sort of aftereffect of the seizure I had last night? Rosie had a seizure too. Is she off somewhere, suffering the same symptoms as me? Rosie. She could be back at any moment. I've got to keep my head in the game.

No, my mind whispers. Rosie won't be back any moment. She snuck out of camp this morning with that bastard Carlos, and the note said they'd be gone at least one night. I have a whole day and night here before I have to shoulder my responsibilities. Might as well enjoy it.

Enjoy it? I can't believe the thoughts my brain is sending me. How can I even think about enjoying a day in 2018, this close to The Collapse, when both I and the person I love are in mortal danger and the situation grows more treacherous by the hour? My eyes flick to Jordan again. She's in just as much danger as Rosie and me. More, in fact, because she knows nothing about what's coming and isn't prepared at all. My lips press into a firm, thin line. So? What do I care?

Jordan bends over to dump a scoop of dirt on the fire and my tongue darts out of my mouth to lick a bead of sweat off my upper lip. For some inexplicable reason, I care a lot.

She straightens up and leans backward with her hands on her hips, stretching her lower back, her hipbones thrusting up over the top of her low-rise shorts. She hooks her thumbs in her front belt loops and bounces lightly on her toes. "Okay, great job, everyone. Who's off work today?"

Several hands go up around the campsite. I raise mine too, not that I imagine Jordan thought I had some sort of job up here.

"Okay," she says. "Now, who's tired of dumpster diving for dinner?"

Every hand in the clearing goes up at that question.

"Me too," Jordan says, looking at various people around the campsite before her eyes fall on me. "Ellen, I'd like you to come with me." She walks over to a tree and grabs two long poles and a box that looks a lot like the one I stole out of Smith Tower, but it's made of plastic, it's bigger, and it's dusty blue with a white lid instead of all black. "We're going adventuring."

A stiff wind blows my hair back from my face and I look out over the vast expanse of choppy saltwater. They try, in The Towers, to keep the color blue alive, but no amount of paint on a wall could ever prepare you for this.

Jordan and I left Scriber Lake and took a bus to the Edmonds waterfront where the land meets an arm of the sea. The still-snowy peaks of the Olympic Mountains make a jagged horizon line far off in the distance. Before I came here to the past, I didn't even know those mountains existed.

I stand on the pier, surrounded by water, and I'm fine. When I first came to the past, the shoreline made me feel sick to my stomach, but that passed quickly. Now, I have no fear of this ocean. I know that it's not the water of my time, and that with my training, I'm its master. I wonder how Rosie feels about it. Did she have the same nervous dread in her stomach that I did for the first few days?

I still don't even know why she's here in the first place. There are so many things I should have asked her father, David Columbia, during the brief time I spent with him two days ago. But he held my life in his hands. And then, in an incredible twist of fate, he offered me the greatest gift of all – a family tie. In an instant, I transformed from an orphan girl from a bad tower to the niece of the most powerful man in the world.

But I was so blown away by his offer, I lost my senses. After becoming his niece, I should have told him immediately why I was here. That General Safeco sent me with the directive to kill a person in Smith Tower on July 2, 2018. He hadn't told me who it would be, just that I would know them when they tried to access a box from the wall on the top floor. I was supposed to kill that person, and then destroy the box and all of its contents.

I was in place and ready. All I had to do was let the arrow fly. Then I'd plunge my return chemicals, come home, and accept my reward. Safeco had promised to appoint me as his successor to lead Safeco Tower, the second most important tower in our world, when I returned from my mission.

But when that mystery assassination target turned out to be Rosie, and I held her life in my hands, I had a split second to decide the fate of the world, and I chose her. I threw away everything Safeco offered me, I chose to stay here, in this doomed past. For her. I had no idea that her father, David Columbia, would offer me something better than Safeco did. I chose Rosie because I love her.

But Uncle David doesn't know any of that. I was too scared to tell him, too scared he'd rip his offer away from me. He thought I'd been sent here by Safeco to save his daughter. I didn't tell him he had it completely backward. Safeco sent me here specifically to kill Rosie and disable David's ability to communicate with her. At the last moment, I found the courage to reveal at least part of the story. I tried to tell him about Safeco's treachery. But he was half-dematerialized when I shouted the terrible truth at him. Did he even hear me?

"What are you thinking about?" Jordan asks in a soft voice.

My god, she moves like an evening breeze. She's right next to me. She could have slit my throat and I'd have died with only the mildest expression of surprise on my face. Maybe this girl would have a better chance of surviving in 2074 than I gave her credit for.

I can't tell her the thoughts in my mind, but I have to say something, so I keep it benign. "The water," I answer.

"What about it?"

"I was wondering if Rosie is scared of it," I say, surprising myself with my own honesty. What is it about this quiet leader standing next to me that seems to have stripped away my guard and has me so reckless?

"Why would she be scared of water?" Jordan asks.

I scan the horizon. Little boats dot the waves. A green-and-white Washington State Ferry pushes west far out over the water. "Things are different where we grew up," I say vaguely.

"Where's that?" Jordan asks.

Why did I open the door to this conversation? My brain searches frantically for something that will make sense in context but give nothing away. "Columbia," I blurt out. God, why did I say that? I suppose it's better than if I'd said 'Wells Fargo,' but not by much.

"Wow, that's in South America, isn't it?"

How would I know? "Yeah," I say. I don't care if it is or not, but if that's what Jordan thinks, I'm not going to argue with her, I'm just going to redirect this conversation as quickly as possible.

"So what, is there no water down there? Does she not know how to swim or something?"

I shake my head. "No, there's water everywhere. It's just a lot more dangerous." *Nice going, Ellen*, I berate myself sarcastically. Not exactly doing a bang-up job of making Jordan lose interest in this conversational thread.

"So, what's the plan? What are we doing here?" I ask her. Better to get her talking so I can keep myself from saying anything else stupid and revealing.

"One of my favorite things," she says with relish. She shakes one of the long sticks in her hand. "We're fishing."

I focus on the stick and see that it's way more than a thin, flexible piece of wood. It's got metal on it. Little loops that hold a thin piece of cord intricately laced through, and some sort of device down near the base, with more cord wound around it.

"Fishing?" I say, unable to keep the questioning lift out of my voice.

"Yes, you've heard of it, right, with all that dangerous water you grew up with?" Jordan says playfully.

Actually, I haven't. But from the tone of her voice, I instantly know it's not something I can admit to. "Of course."

"Have you ever done it?"

I know it's safe to say no to this, so I do.

She smiles. "I can teach you. I've been fishing since I was about this high." She puts her flat palm down near her knee. "It's not for everyone," she continues. "Some people think it's boring."

She kneels and opens the clasp on her scuffed blue-and-white box. She lifts the lid, pulls something out, then secures the clasp again. "This is called a lure."

Using expert, well-practiced motions, she affixes it to the string on the end of her stick. "I wish I had bait, but the ground was so dry back at camp, I couldn't find any worms. I still think we'll pull something in though. I have a great feeling about today."

Strangely, so do I. I breathe in the salt air and watch Jordan's thin fingers dance up and down the pole.

She steps back from the rail. "Do you want to cast?"

"I don't know how."

"I'll teach you."

She gives me the flexible stick and positions my hands above the thing that holds the wound-up string. Stepping behind me, she puts her arms around me to grip my wrists and guide my motions.

There is nothing boring about this.

Jordan shifts her hips and I move mine, following her lead.

My arms go loose and I let her rear my hands back and help me flick the stick. The lure rockets away from the tip of the stick, arcing through the air and plunging under the surface of the water, the thread trailing it. I immediately feel a slight pull as the lure begins to sink, and I instinctively tighten my hands on the stick.

"Well done," Jordan marvels.

"It was all you," I protest.

She keeps her arms over mine and tightens her grip atop my fingers. "You're a fast learner."

I don't argue about that because she's right. It's an essential skill, growing up in The Towers.

"Keep a tight hold, and let me know if you feel a sharp tug, okay? I'm going to cast my own rod."

I'm feeling sharp tugs in a lot of places, but not the kind she means, I'm pretty sure. I don't understand my body right now. Jordan steps away from me and I grip the base of the fishing pole so hard, my hands shake.

She moves about ten feet down the pier, glances back at me and smiles, then shows off, rearing back and flinging her own fishing lure three times as far out into the ocean as mine.

She stands at the railing of the pier, her muscular legs straight, her feet wide apart, knees almost hyperextended. The stiff breeze blows her tangled hair straight back from her face. She looks like a terrible warrior queen, and I can barely breathe.

After a few minutes, she tucks her fishing pole into a notch, shoves her blue-and-white tacklebox against the base to stabilize it, and comes back over to me.

"Any luck?" she asks.

"Nothing yet." I lick my lips. "But I feel lucky today, so I'm not ready to give up." Our eyes lock for several long moments.

"Good," Jordan finally responds. "Fishing is about outlasting your opponent. And ninety-nine percent of the time, your opponent is not the fish."

"Who is my opponent?" I ask, my voice husky and deep.

The question hangs heavily in the air, but before she can answer, two teenage boys come pushing and shoving past us. One of them bangs into me, and he 'catches himself' by digging his clumsy fingers into my butt cheeks.

"Hey!" I shout.

"Hey, yourself," he shoots back. "Don't try and act like you didn't like it."

The boys guffaw and high-five each other.

"Hey, Abercrombie and Fitch, screw off," Jordan snaps.

"Do you know them?" I ask in a low voice.

The taller boy, the one I guess is Abercrombie, shoots his hand out and gooses Jordan. She whirls around swinging, but he's already dancing away. He bounces on his toes and shadow-boxes a couple of punches, laughing.

I shove Jordan behind me, against the railing, and shield her with my body. My fists are as hard as the round end of a ball-peen hammer, and they ache, wanting so badly to hit one of the cackling boys. But which one?

"Oh, I see how it is." Abercrombie sneers. "Coupla rug munch-ers. You're the man, I guess?"

Now I know which one will swallow his own teeth first.

But just as I make a move, the boys zoom in two different directions, as if they telepathically communicated a plan. Fitch, the short one, runs down the dock the way we came, toward the shore. If I go after Abercrombie, Fitch will get away. So I race after Fitch, but I don't get more than a dozen feet before Jordan's piercing scream splits the air.

"No!" she cries. Her sob is filled with such anguish, it sounds like she was gutted. Did Abercrombie stab her in the stomach? I spin on my heel, abandoning the fleeing Fitch, my heart in my throat. I expect to find Jordan's intestines pouring out of her life-less corpse, but physically, she's fine.

She stumbles toward the taller boy, Abercrombie, who has her blue-and-white box raised above his head.

"No, no, no!" Jordan screams. Other people fishing on the dock stare openmouthed at the scene, but no one moves to help her. The boy rears back and heaves the box over the side, then flings her fishing pole in after it.

Jordan reaches him and takes a swing at him, but he's quick and he dances out of the way. Laughing gleefully, he runs farther down the dock, not toward shore, but toward the dead end. It's a long way from here, but he's trapped. He's easy prey, and he might be too fast for Jordan, but he's never met the likes of me.

"Stay here. I've got him." I spit, keeping my eye on him as he dashes down the dock. "Watch out for Fitch."

Jordan sinks to her knees with her hands over her face. Oh my god. She's sobbing.

"Jordan, what did he do to you?" I only planned on beating him senseless, but now, I change my mind. I drop to my knees as well and put my hands on her shoulders. "I'll kill him," I promise solemnly.

"Killing him won't bring it back," she chokes.

"Bring what back? Your fishing pole?"

She shakes her head.

"The box?" I guess.

She raises her tearstained face. "My grandpa gave me that box. He was the only one who...the only one who ever..." She can't finish her sentence. "It's all I had left of him."

I have Abercrombie's face burned into my memory. Fitch too. I'll find them. I'll get the street network on it, just like I did with Carlos. They'll get what's coming to them. But right now, I know what's more important. I'm getting Jordan's box back. And maybe somewhere, in the balance of the universe, it will right the scales a bit and make up for the box I stole.

"I'll get it for you," I say firmly.

With great effort, Jordan peels her hands from her face and

gives me an anguished look. "The water's a hundred feet deep here. At least. That box was full of grandpa's tackle. All his hand-made lures." Her voice cracks and she starts to cry again. "It sank like a stone. It's gone."

I'm already packing my lungs while she's talking. I strip out of my vest and kick off my shoes so I'm down to just my white tank top and denim shorts.

My return chemicals are in that vest. I've never gone more than a minute or two without it on. A small, detached part of my brain doesn't believe I'm doing this, but I'm *definitely* doing this.

"Are you going somewhere? What's happening?" Jordan asks, fresh tears trembling on her lashes.

I thrust the vest at her. "Put this on and keep it safe. I'm getting your grandpa's box back."

She slips her arms in the sleeve holes, seemingly on autopilot. "You can't. There's no way."

I pack a last lungful of oxygen down past my epiglottis. I can hold my breath the third longest among all of my littermates, so I know I can spare the little burst of oxygen it takes to say one more thing. "You've never seen me dive."

I use my upper body strength to push my whole body upward and in one smooth motion, I stand on the dock's railing, my toes curling around the edge.

"What the hell?" someone shouts, but I don't give anyone time to try and stop me. I flex my knees and spring forward. I jack-knife my body, and after a beautiful moment of freefall, I plunge straight into the cold, salty water.

I pop my eyes open and I'm instantly amazed at the clarity of the water, though the salt stings a bit. I talk myself through it. *The salt is good for my corneas; anyone from the towers would give their right arm at an opportunity for a saline rinse like this.*

My arms and legs had moved on autopilot up till now, but something about the phrase 'give their right arm' doesn't sit well with me, though I can't put my finger on why. I pull too hard with my next frog stroke downward, and my arms and legs get out of sync.

This isn't a great time to lose focus, and this time instead of mentally extolling the virtues of a saline rinse, I mentally kick myself in the ass. My arms and legs pull in synchronicity again, pushing past my weird little stumble.

The water is so clean and blessedly free of junk. I don't know for sure what the bottom will be like, but I know it won't be a debris field like I'm used to in tank training. In the towers, in my time, we begin training almost as soon as we're born, but it gets formal around age six. I've done so many climbs and so many deep dives. My dives have always been in tank conditions, though, so I can't get cocky now. Currents were simulated, and while they were tougher than what I'm experiencing now, they weren't natural. I can't underestimate the power of the real ocean for a second.

I've always planned on becoming a welder, so I've focused a lot on metallurgy and chemistry, but it's not like I slept through my coursework on physics, ballast, and buoyancy. I pause my strokes for a moment and let the current push me a bit. I make a minor course correction. If the water is a hundred feet deep like Jordan says, I should reach the bottom in a couple minutes and by then most, if not all, of the ambient light will be gone. The tacklebox was about thirty pounds, but much smaller than my body. At its weight and density, I estimate that the current could have pushed it no more than fifteen degrees off course. With no light to see by, my calculations need to be as precise as possible because I'll be finding this box by feel. I can only hope it didn't burst open and scatter its contents on the way down. I really want to find it and impress Jordan.

A little bubble of my oxygen reserve pops out of my lungs. Did I really just think that? Well, why else would I rescue a plastic box when I should be up top ripping Abercrombie's and Fitch's tongues out of their mouths and flinging them into the ocean?

My hands scrape what feels like rocks. It's pitch black, so I canvass the seafloor in a grid. I come across a foreign object, but it's not the box. It's too big, and it feels like it's made of metal.

There's almost no current down here, so I'm certain my grid pattern is true. The tacklebox has to be nearby. *Not if it busted open*, my mind taunts.

Oh, shut up, I tell it.

I've been down here a while. How many minutes of stored breath do I have left? Five? Six?

I picture Jordan's face when she sees me rise up from the water, her most prized possession in my hands. I kick harder. I must find that box.

And then my fingertips graze plastic. Eagerly, I run my hands over it. Nubby with a funny little swirl pattern. Hinges in the back. Lever-style recessed handle on top. Another bubble of oxygen escapes me. This has to be it.

I lace the fingers of my right hand through the handle, tug, and pull it off the bottom, then hug it to my chest. I can't risk having the handle break off during my swim.

That leaves just my legs to get me to the surface. No problem.

I give the bottom a strong push with my feet and rocket upward, then frog kick. I move up, but not as quickly as I thought I would. In all my training, even in my deep dive simulations, I'd never realized how much stored oxygen increased my buoyancy. Now, with a thirty-pound weight in my arms, only my legs to kick, and ninety feet between me and the surface, I don't have enough stored oxygen to help me rise.

How many more minutes do I have? Three? Maybe? Will that be enough?

It has to be. I'm coming closer to the surface. There's a murky light reaching me now, but how many more feet of water slosh between me and fresh air?

My lungs just begin the first burn. From experience, I know the first burn will last about thirty seconds, then I'll have an almost euphoric second wind that will last maybe a minute, where I'll feel no pain. I'll enter the second burn, where my lungs will feel as if they're imploding, followed by one more brief euphoric period. If I enter the third burn, where black spots appear before my eyes, I'll die.

If I die, I won't save Rosie.

Frack. Am I honestly putting Rosie at risk just to impress a zed?

I kick furiously with my legs, and I shift the weight of the box in my arms. I loop the fingers of my left hand around the handle. I need to pull with my right arm, in addition to kicking. If I drown, no one gets the tacklebox, and Rosie never reunites with her father. Everyone dies.

The water is light enough now that I can see my hand in front of my face every time I reach up to sluice more water past my body as I struggle to surface. When I get back to 2074 I have got to talk to the deep water training coordinator about orchestrating some better simulation dives.

I've entered the second burn when my questing hand breaks the surface. I look up just in time to see the last foot of water sparkle like diamonds above me, then I'm back in the air.

I expel the rest of my stored oxygen, suck in a giant breath, and once more, I hug the tacklebox to my chest. Safe.

I tread water and look around to get my bearings. *Oh, for crying out loud.* The rock wall of the jetty is right next to me. A few feet over and I could have climbed out faster than I swam up.

I gulp in another huge lungful of the crystal clean air and chuff a sardonic little laugh. I clamber onto a rock and rest. I'm not far from the fishing pier, and I scan the length of it, as far as my eyes can see. I count the little metal and plexiglass shelters. We were near the third one. One, two, three, four, five, and I don't spot Jordan at any of them. I climb a little higher for a better vantage point. Still no Jordan.

Did she leave? I thought her grandpa's box mattered to her. I hoped that I – I cut myself off before I finish that thought. Of course I don't matter to her. She's a zed and I'm just someone who considered killing her this morning but didn't.

I should just leave this tacklebox here – what do I need it for anyway? But I don't. Barefoot, I lug the stupid thing over the slippery rocks until I make my way to the top of the jetty then back down to the solid beach. I trudge up the sand, past little kids building castles. The kids ignore me, but the adults with them stare at me in wide-eyed shock.

"You've got something in your hair," one of the zeds calls out. I reach up and pull a rope of seaweed several feet long from the top of my head.

"Ellen!" The scream comes from above me somewhere, and I twist around, my toes digging into the sand. Jordan? It has to be Jordan, doesn't it? The only other girl I know in this time who knows me as Ellen is currently MIA with Carlos.

My eyes find her. She's at the top of the stairs that lead to the beach, standing with a knot of people carrying clipboards.

I feel a smile split my face, and a small part of me is alarmed at how happy I am to see her, but I squash that thought and hurry up the beach while she rushes down the stairs toward me. When she reaches me, she doesn't stop, instead plowing into me and throwing her arms around me.

"Careful. The tacklebox." I gasp as it nearly slips out of my grip.

"You went underwater for fifteen minutes, and you're telling me to be careful?" Jordan screeches.

I thought she'd be happier.

She takes the box out of my hands, stares at it, then hugs it tightly to her chest. She's still wearing my silvery vest. "I thought you were dead. I can't believe you actually got it."

"For you."

"What?"

"I didn't just *get it*," I say, staring hard at the sand under my feet. "I got it for you. Specifically."

Jordan sets the box down on the beach, puts her foot on top of it, takes my face in her hands, and kisses me.

This isn't my first kiss, but it's the first time it hasn't been weaponized, used as a tool to get what I want. Now, the only thing I want is for this moment to never end. I put my foot on the tacklebox as well, wrap my arms around her waist, and kiss her back.

CHAPTER ELEVEN

July 7, 2018 – David Columbia

"Oh, it's you. Welcome back."

David nods and grimaces, which is as close as he can get to the pleasantry that he knows is expected.

"A small drip coffee, I presume?"

"That's right." David grunts.

The man pours him a cup. "$2.35," he tells David.

David pushes a five-dollar bill across the counter, grabs his coffee, and trudges to the farthest table, the one in the corner where two edges of the window meet in a fusion of glass. There, with his back to the window, he can survey the entire establishment, all the way past the mural and to the elevators.

He'll order a new coffee every two hours and pay with a five, leaving the change as a tip for the server. It's not the extravagant tip he sometimes offers when he wants to be left alone because he's certain that a ninety-seven dollar tip every one hundred and twenty minutes would draw far more attention than he's in the market for.

Today will be his third day camping out at the coffee shop on the fortieth floor of Columbia Tower, and he never thought he'd be capable of growing tired of a hot drink, but he finds himself in exactly that situation now. Tonight, after the coffee shop closes, David will venture downstairs to grab a bite to eat. He'll sleep on the streets, and if anyone bothers him, they'll regret it.

How many more days will he spend like this, uselessly sucking down coffee, nerves strung out on caffeine, waiting for his daughter and Ellen to arrive?

As many as it takes. Patience is the only tool left in his arsenal. All of his faith rests in Ellen's ability to track Rosie and that bastard Carlos, who kidnapped her.

Ellen has a street network – sources, people on the ground she can lean on to find Carlos and recover Rosie. How long has she been here that she could develop such extensive contacts? He knows Safeco sent her here to save Rosie, but he knows no details beyond that.

David's hands tighten around his coffee cup so suddenly, the lid pops off. General Safeco is a traitor. He's the one who issued the abort command for Rosie's trip, sending her back upstairs and past the no-man's floor. That's what enabled Sarah, Rosie's stepmother, to waylay her and push her down an open, flooded elevator shaft.

But now a new thought squirms into David's mind, one that hasn't occurred to him before. If Safeco was an accomplice to the murder attempt on Rosie in 2074, why would he send Ellen on a mission to 2018 to save her?

David rises abruptly from his table and stalks over to the counter, pushing his way past two other men in line. The barista wrinkles his brow and checks his own heavy gold wristwatch. He's grown accustomed to David's prompt schedule of a new coffee every two hours, and it's been nowhere near that long since the last time he served him.

"Can I help you, sir? There is a bit of a line."

"I need paper – and a pen." David says gruffly.

The barista tilts his head, and David imagines that he's mentally calculating how much David has tipped him over the last two and a half days. Apparently, it's enough. The man in the green apron plucks a pen out of a jar full of coffee beans and hands it to David, then sets the empty paper cup and the Sharpie he'd been holding down on the countertop. "Let me check in the back for paper. We should have something."

The men in line behind him huff but don't say anything. David stares at the Sharpie laying on the countertop. Is that the same one Rosie used to scribble her hasty cry for help on the mural? David reaches toward it, his fingers trembling, as if he might somehow psychically connect with her by touching the same object.

The barista returns through a swinging door and David snatches his hand back. The man passes David a top-bound lined notepad. "Use as much paper as you need," he offers. He picks up the empty cup and thick black marker. "Next?"

David returns to his table, again sits with his back to the windows, and hunches over the paper, scribbling madly with the ballpoint pen. He pours out everything he can remember about the last six weeks of his life. Some of that time was spent in 2074. Some of it passed here, in 2018. A bit of it was in 2069, and he and Safeco had a conversation there. Is that relevant? David sets the pen down and rubs his face with both hands. Who knew what, and when? The timing is critical. He wishes Lisa were here to make sense of the timeline. Her keen memory and reassuring presence would help.

David tips his head back, letting it bump softly against the window behind him. It's not Gila-shielded now, but it doesn't need to be yet. David's eyes pop open. But it should be soon. He leans forward and steeples his hands together. The Collapse is, what? Nine and a half months away? A bit less? Where are the workers bustling to prepare the building for the chaos that's in store? Hasn't his mother started by now?

David folds his arms on the tabletop and buries his head in them. Good god. His mother, Rosarita. He hasn't thought of her in ages. Before all this, she crossed his mind daily. How he could use her guidance and her sharp mind now. Her voice, permanently hoarse from smoke inhalation she suffered while fighting a tower fire in the early days, whispers in his mind. *Don't forget to journal it, David. Everything always makes more sense when you see it in writing.*

He takes a deep breath through his nose, lifts his head, and grabs his pen again. His mother has never been wrong. His pen moves again, recording memory after memory. He's not sure he has all the details right, but as he scribbles on the page, he finds a clarity that has been missing this entire time. He's read Lisa's notes, back in the travel chamber in 2074, the debriefs of all of his missions, but none of it has been as revealing this one long stream of consciousness rant on the page.

When he finally exhausts his thoughts, he's filled fifteen pages in tiny, cramped handwriting. He looks up and clutches the sides of his head. Looking at no one in particular, David speaks aloud. "Safeco sent Ellen here to kill Rosie."

Behind the counter, the barista drops something large and metallic, and a gonging sound rings out across the café, punctuating David's thought. As the metal clang reverberates around the room, bouncing off the glass windows, David sits with his mouth hanging open, his eyes staring wide.

Ellen came here to kill Rosie, not save her. David is certain of it. But she didn't do it. She failed her mission.

But why? Ellen gave David enough details, days ago when he surprised her in the bunker, to convince him that she'd seen Rosie and observed her at close range. Ellen could have used any number of methods to murder Rosie here in the past. But she hadn't.

And she's out there, right now, trying to find her. Supposedly. She gave him the slip to do it. Why? If she had nothing to hide, why hadn't she met him when she was supposed to? Four hours was all she needed to wait, but she'd vanished during that time, leaving him only a cryptic note.

He revisits the message in his head, this time, viewing it through a new lens. Ellen's last line – 'Tell him about Lita or I will' – stands out to him now. David still doesn't know what it means, but it gives him something he can sink his teeth into, something he can do besides suck down coffee on the fortieth floor of Columbia Tower while he waits for his daughter to be delivered to him by the girl sent here to kill her. Rosie is in more danger than ever, and it's not just the approaching Collapse she has to fear.

David needs to find out who this Lita person is, and he needs to do it now. There is no Lita in 2074, he's certain of that. She exists here in 2018, and she may hold the key to his daughter's disappearance. Now, he just has to find her. Ellen created a street network in 2018. So can he. David drains the last dregs of his coffee and crumples the cup in his hand. He won't be getting a refill.

CHAPTER TWELVE

July 7, 2018 – Rosie

"This can't be the right place." Carlos's voice is barely a whisper.

"It's the address Evelyn gave you," I answer, but I understand what he means. This house we're parked outside of reminds me of the place Rosarita Spencer – the woman I mistakenly thought was my grandmother – lived in in Woodway. From everything Carlos has told me about Fast Eddie Fitzgerald, he shouldn't be surrounded by such splendor.

Carlos pushes the foot pedal of the blue minivan we borrowed from Evelyn, engaging the brake, and he's halfway out the driver's door before he remembers to reach back in and grab the keys out of the ignition. He's moving like he's surrounded by a thick fog, though the day is still sunny and warm.

I hop out of the passenger seat and hurry around the outside of the car. I take the keys from where they dangle in Carlos's hand and stuff them in my front pocket.

"Come on," I say, taking his hand, and he follows me quietly to the porch, the confusion on his face warring with another emotion smoldering on a low burn in his eyes.

I ring the bell. A moment later, I hear a chime echo beyond the closed double doors. Instead of the sound of shuffling feet approaching to greet us, however, I hear a voice coming from the direction of the ring-box.

"Who are you? What do you want?" the voice asks, and Carlos seems to snap out of his fugue state.

"Eddie? It's Carlos Alvarez. Arturo Alvarez's son. Evelyn sent me. Do you remember me?"

The voice remains silent, but I'm sure it came from that ring-box. It's like a tiny little comm. I put my face close to it and try to find the speaker.

"Hey, back up," the voice blasts at me. "It's not you I'm tryna look at."

Instead, I get even closer. How can such a loud voice come out of a tiny little box on the wall, from a comm speaker I still haven't found?

Carlos puts his hand on the small of my back and gently guides me away from the mini-comm. He takes my place, putting his face close to the box.

"Losi?"

When Evelyn called him 'Losi' Carlos seemed to like it, but this time, his fists curl into balls and tremble. I don't know if the guy on the other end of the camera can see that, though, because the tone of his voice doesn't change. "Is that really you?"

"It's me," Carlos says.

"What are you doing here?"

Carlos glances over his shoulder at me and blinks rapidly, then looks back at the camera and lies. We didn't plan this, so I'm kind of surprised by what he says, and I do my best to keep a neutral look on my face. "My girl wants to get a job at a nursery. She's real good with plants, but the place she's applying at has some – uh – specialized equipment that she needs to know better before she goes in for an interview. I thought you could help her with some of her questions."

There's a long pause on the other end of the weird ring-box speaker, then there's a click from the door. "Step inside, and wait there."

Carlos straightens, but his good posture doesn't go all the way to his shoulders. They stay slumped forward a little. I slide my hand into his. "Thank you." I squeeze his fingers. "I know this is hard for you."

Carlos bends, I think to kiss me on the cheek, but he just brushes his lips near my ear and whispers. "Don't mention my feelings. Ask your questions and then we're out of here."

I swallow hard and let Carlos pull me through the front door and into the entryway.

We're not there long before a man approaches us. For a split second, I think it must be Eddie, but then Carlos says, "Who are you?"

"Security. Arms out to your sides."

Carlos's lips part, but he does as the man ordered, so I do too. If this guy tries anything funny, I can disable him in nine different ways, but he just runs his hands over the outside of our bodies, checking for weapons the way I've seen Dad's guards do a thousand times, so it's not a big deal to me.

The large man sniffs, rubs his nose with the back of his hand, and turns his face to the chandelier above us. "All clear," he announces, and now I know where the camera in this room must be hidden.

He puts his hand to his ear, and I notice a little device coiled around his ear flap. Two litter cycles before mine, ninety percent of the children were born partially deaf; we don't know why. On my third trip to the past, Dad had me steal a hundred and fifty hearing aids. That's sort of what this thing looks like, except it's a little bigger. I think someone must be talking to him through it, and I make a mental note to look into that technology. If it's battery operated, that could be really useful to us in 2074.

I have to remind myself that I'm not going to back to 2074. Ever. I close my eyes and breathe deeply. My forehead twinges just a bit, and maybe...I think I might have a new memory. I squeeze my eyes shut harder and hold my breath, thinking. My dad's in a helicopter, and he's shouting, with his hand over his ear. Did it work? Do we have those now? The hearing-aid-communication-device thingies?

"Come with me," the man says, interrupting my thoughts, and my stored breath bursts out of me in a huff. I can't devote my energy to anything but grilling Fast Eddie Fitzgerald right now. I'll explore my mind for new memories later.

Carlos takes my hand and we lace our fingers together while we walk down a long hall and into a sunken living room.

With a sharp intake of breath, Carlos drops my hand and crosses to the far wall. He stands in front of a honey-colored wood contraption hanging on the wall. Six little knobs poke out of the skinny end. Wires wrap around them and stretch the length of the device, terminating at a flat metal clip or something. I join Carlos at the wall and stand at his side, examining the apparatus too, wondering what its purpose is, and why Carlos is so enthralled with it.

"You see I kept it," a voice behind us says. It's not a nice voice, but it's not mean, either. It's just flat and matter of fact.

Carlos doesn't turn around, maybe because he's transfixed by the thing on the wall, but I can't stand having my back to some unknown person, so I turn around and give the new man in the room a long look up and down. He's much shorter than I expected him to be. Half a foot shorter than Carlos, at least. His face matches his tone of voice: flat and expressionless. His eyes are naturally narrow, and I can't tell what color they are. All I can see are little pinprick pupils.

"Hello, Eddie," Carlos says, matching Eddie's flat tone.

Eddie nods, a quick little bobble, and corrects Carlos. "Edward."

Now Carlos finally turns around. "Oh, right. Evelyn told me."

"And who is this?" Eddie says, motioning to me.

"This is Rosie." Carlos claps a heavy hand on my shoulder.

I wiggle gently from Carlos's grasp, then step forward and hold my hand out to shake the way I know civilized people are supposed to. Eddie gets a smile on his face that makes me think of the word 'ingratiating.'

"I understand you're the reason for this little reunion." Eddie shakes my hand with an iron grip.

"Yes," I say. For a second, I'm tempted to tack a "sir" on the end of my statement, the way I would if I were talking to my dad or one of his guards, but I decide against it. 'Sir' is too big a sign of respect and would immediately put me in a subservient position, and that's not where I want to be relative to this guy.

Eddie releases my hand and laces his fingers together but leaves his index fingers free and taps them against his front teeth. "I thought, now that Carlos is an adult, he might have reasons of his own for this reunion."

"I've been an adult for over a year," Carlos says. "And I've been just fine, thanks. I don't need anything."

Eddie turns his hands out so that his pointer fingers are facing us and he moves them in a pincer motion. It's almost like he's pantomiming a gun, but not quite. "I've had a few people stop by in the last couple years who maybe didn't have the best of intentions, weren't really here to catch up. I've had to take some precautions," he says.

"I can imagine some people might want to ride the wave of your success," Carlos says carefully.

"Yes," Eddie says. He throws his head back and laughs, a deep belly laugh. "It's good to see you, Losi."

"Carlos," Carlos says evenly. Eddie's eyes get even squintier.

He tilts his head at an angle. His eyes are so thin, they look closed, but I know he's appraising Carlos through those slits.

"Not a little boy anymore, are you?" Eddie says finally.

"No. I haven't been for a long time."

Eddie seems to come to some sort of decision, and he nods briskly. "Good then. I'm glad I kept this safe all these years."

He crosses the room, passes us, and lifts the wooden thing off the hook it hangs from. He holds it out, offering it to Carlos. "This is yours."

I don't know what the thing in Eddie's hands is, but I can tell it's special to Carlos because his eyes widen and his chest ceases moving. Carlos reaches for it, holding it by the skinny end, then cradles the whole thing to his body. "Thank you."

Eddie nods, and it's as if ten thousand unspoken words have passed between them and I don't know what any of them are, but the vibe in the room has shifted from two predators silently circling each other to those same predators sitting with their heads cocked. It's slightly more comfortable, but just barely. "Do you play?" Eddie asks.

"Not much. But maybe I'll learn."

"Arturo would be proud."

Eddie says that as though Carlos's father is dead, and Carlos obviously picks up on it. "I hope he will be," Carlos says evenly.

I have to jump in now, or these guys are going to go right back to mentally eviscerating each other. "Carlos tells me you can answer questions I have about hydroponics."

Eddie focuses his slit eyes on me now in a way that he hadn't before. I know that look on his face; I've seen it a million times in The Towers. He's judging me, figuring out my angle, looking for weaknesses. He's a predator, but I'm no one's prey, and I match his stare with an intensity of my own.

"You don't need a deep understanding of hydroponics to stock plants at the hardware store." Eddie tilts his head to the side and sneers.

"It's a bit more extensive than that." I match his acidic tone drip for drip. "Specifically, I have questions about static solution culture, passive sub-irrigation, top-fed deep water culture, and rotary systems."

Eddie's eyebrows rise and his eyes are finally open enough to reveal icy blue irises. "I wouldn't recommend rotary. Plant's gonna put more energy into fighting gravity than producing quality product."

"But the plants mature faster and you can grow more in a small footprint."

"You go rotary, then I don't have to worry about you competing against me on quality," he says smugly.

"You don't have to worry about me competing against you at all," I snap back. "I can absolutely guarantee you that my interest in this is non-commercial."

"Oh, see, that's surprising because Carlos said you needed the info to get a job," Eddie says, a 'gotcha' note in his voice.

I purse my lips and look Eddie up and down. I can feel Carlos's tension radiating off his body at my side. When Eddie and I lock eyes, I know what to say. "Carlos was misinformed."

Eddie crosses his arms over his chest and barks something halfway between a cough and a laugh. "You've got yourself a little firecracker here," he says to Carlos.

"Yeah. She likes to blow shit up all the time." Carlos clenches his fists.

Inwardly, I wince. Eddie I can deal with. It's Carlos who's the wildcard now. I turn to Eddie. "This isn't really Carlos's thing. Do you have an office where we can meet and I'll go through my list of questions? Carlos can wait here."

Beside me, Carlos stiffens as if he's transformed to wood.

"Yes," Eddie says smoothly. "Carlos can wait right here with Dmitri. Watch some TV. Have a soda."

Eddie is treating Carlos like a little kid and I get the sense that he's reveling in it. I hate that I'm shoving Carlos into this backseat position, but I need this information and he's not helping.

"Rosie," Carlos says, warning in his voice, but I cut him off.

Turning, I place my hand in the middle of his chest, palm flat. I want to feel his heartbeat and it's a gesture that's meant to be reassuring to both of us, but instead it comes off like I'm holding him back and pushing him away. "I won't be long."

Carlos sucks in his breath, and I'm sure he wants to say something, but he bites his lip, turns from me, and stomps over to a brown leather couch. He sits stiffly on the edge, balances the apparatus he's still holding across his knees, and glares at me. "Do it then, Rosie. But remember. This is it. Get it out of your system because we're not coming back to Bremerton."

I break eye contact with him. If Eddie has the kind of information that I think he might, then it's going to be up to me whether I return to Bremerton. With or without Carlos's blessing.

Eddie and I talk shop for thirty minutes or more, and it's as I suspected. He is a key piece of the hydroponic puzzle. I learn more about indoor farming in half an hour, talking to Eddie, than I had in five years of routine floor maintenance. I learn details about initial install that no one knows because none of our people were around to see the equipment go in. I also have a list of suppliers, companies and websites that I can order large-scale equipment from. I still have no idea how I'm going to pay for any of it or where I'm going to have it shipped, but one thing at a time, I guess.

Eddie's squinty eyes are almost always at half-mast, but he's barely keeping them open now, and I can tell he's getting bored. I need to wrap it up. One more question, and I'm out. Just as I open my mouth, Eddie's pocket starts to buzz.

He jerks in his seat and grabs a phone out of the front pocket of his jeans. His tiny eyes pop open. "I have to take this."

Hunching away from me, he presses the phone against his ear. "I told you not to call me until it was done," he seethes. He listens intently for a few moments, high spots of color appearing in his formerly bloodless cheeks. "Goddammit," he snarls. "What kind of shit are they trying to pull here? If they don't have bump stocks, I don't want 'em. What do they think I want 'em for, a charity fox hunt?"

Seated across from Eddie, I hear Carlos's voice in my mind. *"He was into way more stuff than just growing pot. Illegal gambling, for one. I think he fenced guns..."* I lurch involuntarily as I put two and two together and realize what this must mean.

Eddie's eyes zoom at my movement. He snaps his fingers twice in the direction of my face. "Step out in the hall and wait for me there. Do not wander my residence."

My mind racing, I stride across the room and out the door. I close it behind me and sink to my heels, my back pressed against the wall. Of course I'm not going to meander off. Because this creepy guy is more than just the key to feeding my people, he's the muscle that makes it happen.

No one handed over Columbia Tower to my grandmother. I drop my head into my hands. Not my grandmother. *Me.*

In the chaos that's coming, no one automatically looks to me to lead. I'm a teenager, and a teenager with a baby at that. I know my history. No one gives me the run of Columbia Tower just because I happen to be the one who prepared for it.

I take Columbia Tower by force.

Eddie's part in this is bigger than I realized. He does more than provide the knowledge I need to feed my people for the next fifty years. He's also going to provide the huge stash of weapons that makes my rise to power possible in the first place.

Carlos dislikes and distrusts Eddie, and I agree that he's sketchy. But I can't worry about Carlos's personal preferences anymore. I must prioritize my people and start to move the pieces into place to guarantee their survival. I need Eddie's shady skills and connections.

Eddie doesn't have to know about The Collapse. I don't plan to tell him. But I just thought of something I can offer him in exchange for a steady supply of weapons. Something he won't refuse.

When Eddie swings the door open a few seconds later, I pop to my feet so quickly, my knees make a cracking sound.

I know what I need to talk about to get this ball rolling, but I'm not sure how to start the conversation.

I don't get a chance to say anything, though, because Eddie is fuming and short tempered. "That's it. We're done here," Eddie says, stomping down the hall.

"But I still have questions," I blurt out, hurrying to catch up with him.

"I've given you more time than I should have. I've got a business to run. This isn't a charity and I ain't Google."

Damn it. I can't let this guy slip through my fingers. Who else am I going to find who can and will supply me with the thousands of weapons that I know I stockpile before The Collapse?

We reach the living room, and I'm still wracking my brain on how to broach what I have in mind to my completely unreceptive audience, when Carlos and the guard Dmitri solve my problem for me. They're watching baseball.

"Hey, Carlos, your girl had some interesting questions, but my time is limited and I need to get back to work. Don't be a stranger." Eddie's tone betrays an opposite wish. I can tell he's hoping he'll never see us again, but I can't let that happen.

My heart swells, but I don't have time to even say a brief, silent prayer of thanks that Carlos is a sports fan. I close my eyes and focus on what the broadcaster is saying. It takes me ten seconds, but I lock on to a few key phrases and begin mouthing the announcer's words, following his speech pattern until I'm sure I have the right game loaded into my mind.

"Cruz's gonna foul off the next four pitches, then strike out," I say.

All three men in the room turn their attention to me.

"What did you say?" Eddie asks.

"I said Cruz's going to foul off the next four pitches." My eyes flash to the screen as the pitcher winds up and the batter sends it hooking down the left field line. "Make that three. Then he's going to strike out."

The room falls silent as we all watch the television screen. I'm in awe. I've heard these games all my life, but I've never seen them. The red pitcher's mound, the dusty batter's box with the scuffed white chalk, the dirt-stained knees of the batter, the impossibly green, impeccably manicured field. They don't talk about that stuff in the broadcasts, and it doesn't look like I imagined it would, but it's amazing. I keep mouthing along with the announcer's words to keep my place in the game as we silently watch the batter foul off three more pitches and then strike out.

"Lucky guess," Eddie says.

"The next batter hits a home run on a three and one count," I say, my voice coming out in a rush.

Eddie raises one eyebrow while Carlos opens and closes his mouth several times in a row. Dmitri stands with his arms folded across his chest, a wall of silence.

"Oh yeah?" Eddie says, his eyebrow still cocked, a note of mild interest in his voice.

"Yeah. They'll measure it at three hundred eighty-one feet," I say evenly. Our only entertainment in The Towers is a repeating loop of old sports and news broadcasts from the last few months before The Collapse. I've listened to them so many times, I've memorized them. And it's about to pay off.

Eddie lifts both his eyebrows now, nods almost imperceptibly, and trains his squinty eyes on the television.

The pitcher winds up and lets the baseball fly. Curveball, eighty-two miles an hour, in the dirt. Ball one.

Eddie glances over his shoulder at me, and I'm not sure if I stop mouthing the words in time or if he catches me, but he turns back to the TV.

The pitcher licks his fingertips, rubs his hand in his back pocket, pulls the ball out of his glove, and lets it fly. Fastball, high and outside. Ball two.

The catcher lobs the ball back to the pitcher, who kicks the dirt on the mound and spits. He fingers the ball, rolling it around in his hand. On the television screen, he has the glove up, shielding his nose and mouth from view. That's a detail I never knew. But I know what happens next. The next ball is way high and outside and gets away from the catcher, but it doesn't really matter because there's no one on base. Ball three.

It's the fifth inning, and the coach is obviously concerned about his pitcher's longevity, as he should be. Everything falls apart for him in just a few minutes. But no one knows that but me. For everyone else in this room, the game is happening in real time.

The coach and the pitcher have a few quick words, the pitcher nods, and the coach trots back to the dugout. The pitcher winds up and burns a perfect strike right down the middle. It's a three-one count.

Carlos, Eddie, and Dmitri all stare at me. I shrug. "I told you."

The pitcher spares almost no time after getting the ball back from the catcher. He winds up and sends a fastball straight down the middle again, but the batter is ready. He puts his weight on his back leg, rears, and swings, connecting with a smack and sending the ball soaring.

"My, oh my, that one is outta here," the announcer crows, and I can't help myself from whispering the last few words.

"How many feet did you say that was?" Eddie snaps.

"Three hundred eighty-one," I say, doing the best I can to keep a smug note out of my voice. I know that everything is riding on this, but I can't help but enjoy it just a little tiny bit.

"The lucky fan who picks up that ball is gonna need to write three-eight-one on it because that's what they're measuring it at," the first broadcaster says gleefully.

"What a monster ball," the other announcer cries. "Tore the leather off that one."

Eddie wheels on me. "How did you know that would happen?" Before I can say anything, he turns to Dmitri. "This is DVR. It must be."

"Nope. Live TV." Dmitri grunts. He picks up a rectangular box off a low table and points it at the screen, apparently doing something to prove to Eddie that what we're watching is happening in real time.

"What happens next?" Eddie says, a note of excitement creeping into his voice.

"He strikes out the next batter, but then Gonzales hits a single, steals a base on a wild pitch, Cano's double drives him in, and then Gordon hits another home run. Healy fouls out to end the inning." I smile pleasantly. "Well, it's been nice talking to you and thank you for everything you shared with me about hydroponics – it was really helpful. Carlos? Are you ready?"

"Wait," Eddie says urgently. "Can you do that, like, whenever you want?"

I shrug. "Basically."

"But…how?"

Oh, crap. I hadn't quite thought that one through. What am I going to say?

Luckily, Carlos comes to my rescue. "She's clairvoyant," he says.

"Like, ESP?" Eddie's beady eyes grow as round as the glass beads that sometimes pummel down on The Towers during a particularly bad storm.

I don't know what ESP is, but I smile and try to look modest.

"Something like that." I have Eddie on the hook now, and I know that he will be more than happy to receive me the next time I come back – alone. "It's getting pretty late, Carlos. I'm ready to head out." I start walking in the direction of the front door, like I own the place and talk casually as all three men follow me. "Oh, and Eddie, if you want to bet on the game, in the top half of the sixth inning, it's three up and three down. Bottom half, they score two more runs before the pitcher gets pulled with bases loaded. One run comes in on a sacrifice bunt, then the next batter grounds out into a double play. Long story short, Mariners win nine to two. Thanks again for your hospitality. I learned a lot."

I click the heavy door shut behind me and Carlos, but the thick sturdiness of the fine-grained wood isn't enough to mask the sudden exclamation from within. "Dmitri!" Eddie shouts. "Call my bookie!"

"What the hell was that, Rosie?"

I stare out the windshield at the oncoming traffic. Carlos drives more aggressively than normally and I wish he wouldn't ride the center line like he is.

"Eddie gave me good information about hydroponics. I thought he deserved some sort of reward." That's not true at all, of course. I was just baiting the hook for the next time I come out here, but I can't tell Carlos that.

"His reward was me not punching him in his goddamn face when his rat fink mouth spoke my father's name."

I take a deep breath. Now is probably not the right time for what I'm about to say, but it's never going to be a good time to speak what's on my mind. "Carlos, I'm really sorry about what happened to your dad. It sucks. It truly does. It's horrible that he's in jail and it's terrible that you and your brother were left to drift like flotsam and jetsam. It's awful how your foster parents used you and how hard everything in life has been for you because of it. But, Carlos…your dad was an adult. Eddie didn't force him to do anything illegal, did he?

"Well no, but—"

"But he did. He made his own choices and he got caught and I'm not trying to be a jerk, I'm totally not, but you can't blame Eddie for your dad going to jail."

"So, what, you're on Eddie's side now?"

"I'm not on anyone's side," I exclaim. "Except yours, and mine, and the thousands of people who are counting on me to save their lives and don't even know it yet."

Carlos jerks the wheel angrily and pulls into a parallel parking spot on the street. He jabs the e-brake with his foot and grips the steering wheel so tightly, his knuckles whiten.

"What, you're just going to park and pitch a fit?" I say. I'm under so much stress and I don't have time to manage Carlos's feelings about this situation anymore. I need Eddie's knowledge, his guns, and I'm pretty sure I need his gambling connections. If he can make money off my sports predictions, then so can I. "I'm sorry that I have to be the one to tell you that your dad's not a victim in this scenario, but you should have been able to figure that one out yourself," I say, my tone harsh. "The only victim was you."

The silence between us is deadly. Finally, Carlos speaks in a tight voice, as cold and sharp as an icicle. "I parked because this is where my brother lives. I wanted to you to meet him – up until now."

Up until now. Oh, god. Here Carlos was, about to introduce me to his younger brother, the person he loves most in the world, and I'm accusing him of throwing a tantrum.

I bite my lip and clutch the sides of my bucket seat. "I was caught up in what we were talking about. I thought you were too. That's the only reason I said that."

Carlos gets out of the van and slams the door. He strides to the sidewalk on his long legs and stands there, his arms crossed over his chest, a scowl on his face. I scramble out of my seat, bumping my head on the doorframe as I get out of the vehicle. I'm several inches taller than I was yesterday, and I'm not used to my long limbs yet. I join Carlos on the sidewalk, my head aching. I leave way more space between us than I normally would.

Carlos hits a button on the key fob. The door locks click down and the van honks once, causing me to jump. I sidle a step closer to Carlos, and he takes one away from me, keeping the distance between us the same. I ball my hands into fists at my sides. He obviously doesn't want me near him right now, but he won't stop staring at me.

"That's it?" Carlos says after a minute. "That's all you're going to say?"

I dart my eyes around the sidewalk, as if the bicycle chained to the lamppost can tell me what Carlos is expecting me to talk about. "What else am I supposed to say?" I ask, unclenching my tight fists and putting my palms out at my sides.

"I don't know. 'I'm sorry' would be nice," Carlos says sarcastically.

"I *did* say I was sorry," I protest.

"No, you didn't. You said you were caught up in what we were talking about and you thought I was too and that's the only reason you said that, about me pitching a fit. You never said you were sorry."

Heat rises in my cheeks. He's right. I feel sorry, but that's different. I never said it out loud. But I'm angry too, and I'm freaking out from the weight of the world on my shoulders, and I can't stand that Carlos is trying to guilt me into giving up the only lead I have on everything I need to safeguard my people. "I am sorry, Carlos. It was a shitty thing to say and I didn't mean it. But you have to understand. I am Rosarita Columbia." I throw my hands in the air. "*Rosarita Columbia!* I'm responsible for the lives of more than fifty thousand people. I'm the only person standing between humanity and an extinction-level event. You can't possibly imagine the pressure I'm under." I take a step closer to him again, and this time he doesn't withdraw, but he still has an expression on his face like he just stepped on a rusty nail.

Tetanus boosters! I almost groan aloud as the thought of stepping on a nail makes me think of another thing I need to stockpile. I can't fall down that shaft of thought now, though, or I'll go insane right here on the sidewalk. My hand trembles a little as I reach toward Carlos and place my hand lightly on his tense forearm. "Can I still meet your brother?"

Carlos pauses a half second longer than I'm comfortable with, but then he shrugs. "I guess." He turns and walks toward a three-story gray building a block ahead, my hand falling off his arm like a dead leaf.

I guess. I trudge after him. This should be one of the happiest moments of Carlos's and my relationship. I should be holding his hand and be gazing at him all dewy-eyed. Instead, I keep my balled fists in my pockets and I stare down at my feet plodding one after the other. There are no surging, churning floodwaters here, but I still feel like a convicted criminal walking toward the edge of a roof, seconds from being thrown off.

CHAPTER THIRTEEN

July 7, 2018 – Ellen

I roll onto my back, immediately missing Jordan's warmth, but I can't hold her in my arms anymore. I have too much to think about.

The last four hours have been the most incredible in my life. It was only when Jordan drifted into a light doze that I pulled my head out of the misty brilliance of cloud nine and came crashing back down to rock-hard earth.

When Jordan kissed me on the beach, my brain went blank. My memories stopped recording like my heart knew what I was doing would tear me to shreds later.

All I recall since Jordan and I began kissing on the beach is input I received from my senses. A delicious shudder passes through me as I relive the silky feel of Jordan's hair in my hands, the sweet scent of her breath on my neck, the salty taste of her skin, the breathless noises she made when we somehow found our way back to camp and burrowed inside her tent.

But now Jordan sleeps lightly, my mind has snapped back into gear, and I'm utterly horrified with myself. Carlos and Rosie could have poked their heads in and asked the time and I wouldn't have noticed or cared. I've been consumed by the mission General Safeco sent me on for over a year. Rosie hasn't been out of my waking mind for even a minute…until now.

I grasp the blankets Jordan and I lay tangled in, pull them higher up my chest, and roll onto my side. My movement wakes her, and maybe I meant it to. Light fingertips trail along my bare arm, raising goosebumps.

"I still can't believe you dove to the bottom of the ocean for me," Jordan whispers huskily. "Superhero."

I keep my body turned away from hers, and she spoons into me. "I'm not a superhero," I say morosely. "I've got good lungs is all."

Jordan moves her hand under the blankets and lets it lie across my waist just above my navel. "You were down there over ten minutes." She presses her flat palm gently against my belly. "I thought you drowned. I'd call that more than just good lungs."

I raise one shoulder in a shrug. "Anyone can do it with enough practice."

Jordan kisses my neck and I can't stay turned away from her any longer. I flip over and stare at her, brushing her hair back from her face with tremulous hands. I must end this now. "Jordan—"

Her brows furrow together and she cuts me off and sits up, pulling the blankets off me and bunching them up around her torso. "No good conversation starts with a first name. You're not about to say 'Jordan, I'm hungry. Let's find dinner,' or 'Jordan, do you have an extra pair of socks I can borrow?' I know you're going to say something shitty, so just say it. Don't try to soften the blow by proving to me that you remember my name."

I swallow. She's got me completely pegged. This girl is nobody's fool and it's so fracking attractive, I can't stand it. My brain feels like it's being whisked like an egg. "Jordan, I… This… This can't happen."

"Too bad. It already did."

I feel my cheeks grow hot, remembering the sensory input. I swallow again. The lump in my throat moves down and it's replaced by an ache of longing. Longing for something I haven't even lost yet. But I can't cave to the temptation of Jordan. The Collapse is coming and Rosie is in terrible danger. I *cannot* give in to my base desires. Again.

I tense the muscles in my neck and say what I have to. "No, I mean, I messed up. Really big."

"For four hours?"

I grit my teeth and close my eyes briefly. This would be so much easier if I could just tell her about The Collapse, and Rosie, and my mission, and everything that's gone wrong, and lay it all out there for her to digest. She would probably think I was crazy, but better have her decide I'm insane than that I don't want her. But I can't. Both General Safeco, traitor that he is, and my new uncle David Columbia have warned me that our entire existence could end in the blink of an eye if I talk about the future. So I'm hamstrung, and I have nothing to say except vague statements. So I blurt one out. "I have obligations. Commitments."

Her upper lip twitches, but she keeps her mouth pressed in a thin line for a moment before she speaks. But when she does, I'm startled by what she says. "It's the same thing every time. I find someone I connect with, I let my guard down, and I find out I'm a side hustle."

"A what?" I say, startled.

"Everyone's heard the rumors about you, Lita. I thought you were different when you said your name was really Ellen and blah blah blah, but I should have listened to my instincts. You're trouble. You maybe thought it would be funny to hook up with me, I don't know. I don't get why you did what you did to get my grandpa's tacklebox back, and it doesn't even matter. I thought maybe it wasn't true that you were with Jimmy Squint, or that maybe you guys broke up or something. I thought maybe…" She shakes her head and throws back the blankets, raising her chin haughtily, unafraid. "But no. Like I said. It's always the same. I'm the second string."

I shake my head, trying not to lose my mind at the beauty of her fury. "I'm not with Jimmy." The thought causes my lip to curl. "He probably gets a lot of mileage out of people thinking we're together, but I fly solo, and even if I didn't…Jimmy? Gross. He has his uses, but when it comes down to it, Jimmy is my bitch. And nothing more."

Jordan chews her lip, the vehemence in my tone undeniable. "Then what is it? What obligations and commitments do you have that make you want to throw away a chance like this?"

"I don't want to throw it away." I ball my fists and press them under my chin. How can I explain this? "But there is someone else," I begin, a note of hesitation creeping into my voice that I did not intend, and Jordan jumps all over it.

"Oh, I see. So there is somebody, but it's not Jimmy, and I'm still a side-chick diversion. Gotcha." She puts her fingers into a sarcastic "okay" sign and flashes it at me. Angrily, she roots around in the blankets and finds her shirt, putting it on inside out.

"No, it's not like that. I mean yes, there's someone else, but shit, I haven't even talked to her in more than a year," I say, my whole body growing stiff and my voice becoming shrill. "And I wasn't looking for anything, but Jordan…" My eyes grow wet and my voice shifts instantly from shrill to hoarse. "Today has been the best day of my life."

What did I just do? Wasn't I trying to break things off? Didn't I start this whole conversation to get Jordan and her distraction out of my life? Now here I am, twisting the whole conversation back around on itself and I'm fighting to win her back. What is wrong with me?

"Oh, baby," Jordan says. "I'm just glad to hear it's a woman. I don't think I can take being left for some dude again." She moves cautiously toward me, reaching with tentative hands to rub lightly across both sides of my ribcage. "Carrying a torch for your ex."

I purse my lips and look down, but I don't correct her. Better for her to think Rosie's my ex than know the truth.

Jordan puts her fingertip under my chin and tips my head back. "You know what?" Her eyes are at half-mast, and she licks her lips.

"What?" I ask, mesmerized by the movement of her tongue.

"I bet I can make you forget all about her."

Jordan leans toward me, her lips parted, and she touches them to mine. She's one hundred percent right. I don't just forget about Rosie. My mind goes blank, like it did before on the beach, and I forget every care, every worry, every concern, every hope, every fear. It all goes away and I feel nothing but the silky softness of Jordan's skin as her body melds into mine once more. Uncounted time races by, bringing us closer and closer to an unavoidable destiny, one that – at the moment – doesn't concern me at all.

CHAPTER FOURTEEN

July 7, 2018 – Carlos

I knew this was a terrible idea. I never should have introduced Rosie to Eddie. That guy was trouble for my family, and now being around him for one measly hour has caused Rosie's heart to harden like a sand dollar left out to bleach at low tide. I'm still kind of in shock over what she said about my dad. I mean, yeah, technically, I guess she's right, but there's technically and then there's reality, and I know, deep down inside, that my dad never would have flashed across the cops' radars if Eddie weren't there hounding him every step of the way. *Grow more, Arturo. My customers don't want ounces – they want pounds. Don't you want to provide for your boys?*

Shortly after Dad got busted, pot became legal in Washington. Now, good men like Dad sit in jail while filth like Eddie rake in money hand over fist and buy mansions. I wonder if he's still running guns and prostitution rings. Legal pot is probably a great way to launder that money. I hadn't told Rosie about any of that.

And now Rosie was giving him sports tips because she felt like she owed him a favor? It was Eddie who owed more than he could ever repay. Dad could have significantly reduced his own sentence by turning state's evidence and ratting out Eddie, but he refused to talk. Carlos understood why Dad kept his silence...and yet...he didn't. Dad's personal code of ethics wouldn't allow him to be a snitch, but it would allow his sons to be thrown to the mercy of strangers as wards of the state? Where were the ethics in that?

But Rosie clearly doesn't understand any of that. How could she? She's Rosarita Goddamn Columbia and don't you forget it.

I pound way too hard on Ricky's apartment door. I open my curled fist, flex my fingers, and knock again, normally this time, so he doesn't think I'm some lunatic trying to beat his door down.

"I'm coming," a muffled voice yells from behind the door, and my heart swells. Rosie might be pissing me the hell off, but seeing Ricky always makes me feel like a million bucks. I rarely come over here to visit because sometimes it's hard for me to pretend like everything's all right and not share what my life is really like. I don't want Ricky to know about me being on the streets or any of the crappy stuff that I've gone through. By the time he ages out of foster care, I plan to have a home for us. Or – better yet – he'll get a full ride college scholarship and then I won't have to worry about putting a roof over our heads for four more years.

Of course, according to Rosie, the world will end before Ricky even attends his junior prom. And I believe her.

Someone throws a deadbolt and the doorknob turns. The door opens two inches, held in place by a thick, gold chain. A boy's brown eye peeks out the crack, growing wide when he registers who's here to visit.

The door slams shut and I hear the hurried disengagement of the chain. Then my little brother flings open the door, shouting my name. "Carlos!"

"Ricky!"

He steps out and engulfs me in a gigantic hug. We embrace for long moments. Good god, can I even call him my little brother anymore? I step back and hold him by the shoulders at arm's length. Yes, I can. I'm still a half an inch taller than him. "You've grown," I exclaim, pressing him into another embrace before I release him for good. "Dammit, man, you're only sixteen! You're gonna end up taller than me!"

Ricky laughs and nods. The last time I was here, he still had vestiges of a little boy in his face, but not anymore. His cheeks have thinned, his nose is larger, and his Adam's apple is pronounced. My little brother turned into a man sometime in the last nine months.

Ricky's eyes flick behind me and his mouth drops open a little bit, and I realize he's just noticed Rosie. "Who's this?" he asks.

I'm still extremely irritated with her, and my response comes out spontaneously. "This is Rosarita Columbia," I say to my brother. "She's very important."

I don't know if Ricky will detect the tinge of snark behind my words, but I know Rosie will, and I hope it gets under her skin.

She acts completely classy, though. "It's really nice to meet you, Ricky. Carlos has told me so much about you." She holds out her hand to shake Ricky's and suddenly I feel like a huge asshole. Yeah, what Rosie said wasn't cool, but why am I so mad? Was it what she said, the way she said it, or the fact that she spoke an uncomfortable truth that I didn't want to hear?

When their hands touch, Ricky remembers his manners and jumps like he got sparked with static electricity. "Oh, hey, you guys don't have to stand out here on the street. Come inside."

"After you, Rosarita," I drawl, trying to relax the mood a little bit. I sweep my arm exaggeratedly in front of myself toward the open door.

She tosses her head with a dignified sniff, throws her shoulders back, and walks into Ricky's brightly lit apartment.

"Sorry it took me so long to get to the door, man," Ricky says. "Though you've got to know that I wasn't expecting you."

"Sorry it's been so long," I say. "Seattle's an expensive city." See, this. This is why I don't come over to visit. I can't lie to my brother. And so far, I haven't. I am sorry it's been so long and Seattle is an expensive city, and I hope that Ricky will assume that means I've been busy working to keep a roof over my head and not ask me too many probing questions about anything. I'm, what, maybe five sentences in to this reunion, and I've already run out of things to say about myself that won't cause him pain and worry.

But this time I have Rosie with me. Maybe we can talk about her. I glance over at her, where she stands with her head bowed, trailing her index finger on something sitting on the kitchen table, examining it. What can I say about Rosie? I can't talk about how we met, how Rosie fell on top of my tent in downtown Seattle, because why would I be in a tent in downtown Seattle? I can't talk about breaking her out of the hospital because that was pretty freaking illegal. I can't talk about staying in Rosie's underground bunker in North Seattle because again, why didn't I stay in my own home, instead of a damp converted tunnel set up like a military-style barracks? Oh, and the person who set it up? Just some guy from the future.

I'm so lost in thought that I'm surprised when Rosie starts a conversation herself. "Is this a communications device?" she asks.

Ricky smiles his shy grin, and suddenly the boy I thought had vanished is back. "Sort of," he admits. "It's just something I've been fiddling with. I haven't got it to work the way I want it to."

"But it's working?" she asks.

"Yeah," he says with pride. "You have to touch these two wires to each other" – he points to a red wire and a thicker white wire – "and you can't twist them together or it blows the whole thing. Just touch them lightly. It's staticky, but I've talked to Adrienne on it when she's been as far as four and a half miles away. It doesn't work at all if it's raining, though."

"Huh." Rosie crouches down on her heels so she can view the contraption at eye level.

"Where is Adrienne?" I ask. Mom's favorite cancer nurse took Ricky in when Dad went to jail so soon after Mom died. She's a licensed foster care provider and she wanted to take us both, but the state said she didn't have enough room and denied her application. I was so worried that they'd tell her she couldn't have Ricky, either, that I said I didn't care. So Ricky stayed with her and I bounced from place to place until I ended up at my last foster home, where I took care of my guardians' disabled daughter until I aged out of the system.

"She's at work. I think she said it was a double."

"Aw, that's too bad." Adrienne's great, but I'm not devastated to miss her. It's one less person to lie to. "Would have been nice to see her. Tell her I came by?"

"Yeah, of course. Are you gonna stay the night? You can sleep in my room with me and, uh…" He blushes and shoots a glance at Rosie. "And Rosarita can, um, well…"

Rosie straightens and looks around the room, at the little curtains with ears of corn on them over the sink, at the recessed canister lighting, at the disassembled vacuum cleaner in the corner – everywhere but at me.

"We probably shouldn't stay," I say. "We'll take the boat back tonight."

Ricky's face falls.

"But we'll stay until the last boat," I say hurriedly, and he sends me a grateful look. I love my little brother. He is the best parts of Mom and Dad and I know he's going to make us all proud. I sling my arm around his shoulder. "So apparently you've invented a new style of Wi-Fi in the kitchen, but that can't be the only thing you've got in the hopper." I point at the vacuum and speak to Rosie in the warmest tone I've probably used with her since we got off the ferry earlier this morning. "This is standard-issue Ricky since the day he was born. Ricky took apart – and put back together – my dad's laptop when he was five. Dad says it actually worked faster once Ricky reassembled it."

Ricky laughs. "He was still mad as a box of frogs, though. I had to stop watching *Bill Nye the Science Guy* and he took away my dessert privileges for a month."

"He'll get a full scholarship to college for sure," I say with pride.

Ricky shakes his head, smiling. "There're a lot of smart kids who want scholarships. I still have to work my ass off for the next two years."

A shadow passes across Rosie's face, and I beg her silently not to get started on her whole "nothing's going to exist in two years" stuff. I guess I should also be happy she hasn't asked "What's college?" She doesn't say anything, but I think Ricky must have noticed the look on her face and misinterpreted it.

"College isn't for everyone, I know, but I think it's the right path for me."

Rosie works to keep her face expressionless, but she just ends up looking pinched, nervous, and kind of pissed, and a silence falls around the kitchen table.

"So, uh, how did you guys meet?" Ricky asks.

Oh, crap. Here we go.

"Carlos got me out of a sticky situation," she says. "I ran into some trouble in downtown Seattle and he came to my rescue. We've been together ever since."

She makes it sound so simple, and I could kiss her for it. I step next to her, take her hand, and squeeze. She looks up at me, her eyes full of questions and sorrow, and I smile down at her. She nestles a little closer and blinks rapidly.

"Classic Carlos. You know, when he was little he founded the Worm Rescue Club at our school?"

Rosie's brow furrows and I feel her stiffen beside me.

"Dude," I say. "Not the same thing."

Ricky's eyes widen almost comically and his jaw goes slack. "I didn't mean it that way. I just meant you've always been a compassionate guy. Jeez. Remember your little sign-up sheet, and how you got like forty people to say that they'd pick up worms on the sidewalk after rainstorms and put them back in the dirt so they could live?" He looks back and forth between me and Rosie. "I'm not making this any better, am I?"

I laugh it off. "Ricky may be a lot smarter than me, but I have way better social skills."

Ricky shoots me an anxious grin. I wanted them to like each other immediately, but walking in here unannounced and in the middle of a fight with Rosie might not have been the best idea.

"You want to see some of the other stuff I've been working on?" Ricky asks.

"Yes," Rosie and I bark in unison. That seems to break the tension a bit, like a sheet of safety glass that's cracked and crazed but won't quite shatter. Given everything we've dealt with today, I guess I should be satisfied with that.

CHAPTER FIFTEEN

July 7, 2018 – David Columbia

David Columbia leans his head against the concrete support beam and sighs. Today was a complete washout. He googled "Lita Seattle" and spent the next few hours winnowing his search terms until he ruled out all of the few seemingly valid leads. As daylight waned and shadows stretched long down the streets, David even tried asking a few zeds, but that had been even less productive. In 2074, David was a skilled leader, capable of getting any information he needed from his people. Here in 2018, however, he's a scruffy man saying "Tell me everything you know about Lita" in an increasingly agitated way.

When a bike cop became overly interested in him, he knew it was time to give up. David popped into Columbia Tower, checked the fortieth floor for Ellen and Rosie just in case, and bought a coffee minutes before the shop closed. Now he's hunkered under the Viaduct, his fingers wrapped around the lukewarm paper cup in his hands, watching the sun dip below the Olympic Mountains to the west.

Should he try again tomorrow? Is there any point? But what else can he do? Giving up is not an option.

A man dressed in tatters shoves an overflowing shopping cart slowly past. David ponders the similarities between this man and a picker from his own time. Sorting through the detritus offered by fate, keeping more than is useful, but unable or unwilling to leave much behind. When you rely on fate to meet your needs, it's hard to turn anything away, even absolute junk. David knows.

On a whim, he calls out, "What's the word on Lita, my good man?" His voice is artificially cheerful and just on the edge of madness.

The man turns his gray, lined face to David. His eyes appear huge behind bottle-thick glasses. "Stay away from that bitch, man. They say she killed ODP. If she did, then you're next." The man laughs hysterically and keeps shoving his cart forward, one of the front wheels bent sideways, slowing him down.

David rockets to his feet, grabs the handle of the shopping cart, and gets right up in the man's face. "Tell me every last goddamn thing you know."

The man bares his yellowing teeth. His gums are so heavily receded that David can see where the roots dive into the man's jawbone. A pocketknife shoots out of the sleeve of his jacket, but David sees that one coming from a mile away and slaps it out of his hand.

"I'm sorry," David says. "I meant, 'Tell me every last goddamn thing you know, *please.*'"

Ten minutes later, when he's satisfied that the cowering man has told him every scrap of information he knows about Lita, David gives him a hundred-dollar bill and tells him to forget they met. An incoming ferry hoots a long, mournful note as it pulls into the dock. David glances at the green-and-white vessel and turns away to walk purposefully uphill. It's going to be a long night in The Jungle.

CHAPTER SIXTEEN

July 7, 2018 – Carlos

Ricky shows us a bunch of different inventions and ideas he's been tinkering with. His brilliance blows me away, but he acts like it's nothing. Like it's just totally normal that a teenage kid from Bremerton would be talking about entropy and closed natural systems and the second law of thermodynamics, or thinking about how to turn hydrogen metallic to make a better electrical conductor. Ricky might be all blasé and downplay his chances of getting a scholarship, but I know it's in the bag. He's excited about an upcoming summer science fair and he spends a ton of time showing us a project he's working on that would extract uranium isotopes from seawater.

Rosie is super interested, of course, because her world is nothing but seawater. I mostly nod and grin and try to ask questions that keep Ricky talking but don't highlight how stupid I am. Ricky got all the brains in the family and I'm proud of my little brother.

My worry that Ricky would find out too much about my life was totally unfounded. Hours pass in a blur and before I know it, it's time to leave. Rosie slips into the bathroom, and I'm pulling my brother in for a hug when he stops me with a sharp look. His brow is knitted and heavy. I'm not used to him looking so somber.

"Carlos, man…are you sure about her?"

"What?" I'm startled by the question. After the rocky start to their meeting, everybody seemed to settle down. Rosie was genuinely interested in his science stuff and asked him tons of questions.

Ricky looks uncomfortable. "You don't think she seems kinda…intense?"

"Takes one to know one, Enrique."

My brother rolls his eyes. "Yeah, but I'm not neurotypical, so I get a free pass."

I punch him lightly in the shoulder. "Shut up."

He jabs me back. "You shut up." We laugh, and for a second it's like we're little kids again, rolling around in the backseat of our dad's Datsun, fighting over who got to play games on our mom's phone.

He grows serious again. "I just want to know that you're happy. I know it's not easy for you. I want you to be with someone who will build you up. You don't have to be Captain Save a Ho."

A floorboard creaks in the hallway and Ricky looks quickly over his shoulder, but it's just the sounds of the building settling as the sun goes down and the air cools off.

"I'm not," I hiss quietly. "She's good for me. You'll just have to trust me on that."

Ricky gives me a skeptical look, and I put my hand on his shoulder. "I'll tell you the whole story another time."

I've been so focused on him, I didn't see Rosie slip back into the room, but I meet her eyes in time to see the alarm flash across them as she absorbs my last few words. I know what she's thinking. She thinks I'm going to give Ricky some sort of insider information on the future and the whole world is going to crumble down around her. Well, doesn't that happen anyway? Isn't that what The Collapse essentially is? How can it get any worse than that? If she thinks I'll let my brother get swept away in a tsunami when I can prevent it, she's crazy. But I know I'm in for a hell of an annoying conversation on the ferry. "Come on, Rosarita," I say resignedly. "Let's go home."

I leave Dad's guitar with Ricky – I can't keep it on the streets – though I don't tell him that. Ricky doesn't remember the guitar like I do. Dad stopped playing when Mom got sick and Ricky was really young then. Even though he has no emotional attachment to it, he promises to keep it safe. Rosie and I drive the van back to Evelyn's and she gives us a ride to the ferry. We don't have to pay a fare traveling in the Seattle direction and the boat is already loading when we get there, so Rosie and I walk right on. She's eerily quiet the whole time.

We're not going to spread our arms out in the evening breeze on the way home. There's not going to be anything romantic about this return trip. Not after the day we've had. I kick myself again for ever bringing up the idea of Eddie. I knew it was a terrible suggestion the moment the stupid words were out of my mouth. I just wanted so badly to be helpful and solve her problems. Maybe Ricky is right. Maybe I am Captain Save a Ho.

I look at Rosie, seated across from me on the navy blue padded bench seat. No. She's many things, but 'ho' isn't one of them. I'm ashamed for even having the thought.

She stares out the window, the glass clouded from years of salt spray. "You know you can't tell him anything, don't you? Ricky, I mean." She speaks so quietly that it takes me a second to even register that she's talking at all.

Her words whip up an instant hurricane of fury inside me. "Oh, so you can give Eddie detailed 'clairvoyant visions' so he can cash in on baseball, but I can't save my brother's life?"

"It's not the same thing," Rosie says through gritted teeth.

"Telling Eddie what's going to happen in a baseball game won't materially affect the future. If you tell your scientist brother that Antarctica's going to flash melt next year, you don't think that could have some serious repercussions?"

"I don't have to tell him the whole story. Just enough to keep him safe."

"And risk the future of humanity?"

"Yes! Though I seriously don't get how me protecting Ricky is any different from you giving Eddie nuggets of information about the near future. I really don't. Because it's the exact same thing. There's no gray area. Eddie is making money he wouldn't have had otherwise. How do you know he's not going to buy something with it that will, I don't know, refreeze Antarctica?"

"Don't be ridiculous. Eddie making more money is not going to shut down a secret nuclear base at the South Pole or cause it not to blow up. And I'm not making random decisions here. I have to give Eddie that information because he knows how to make money off it."

"I'm not following you."

"Don't you get it, Carlos? Rosarita Columbia was supposedly a rich crazy environmentalist or at least that's what we were all told. And I've been sitting here wondering not only how I'm going to get the supplies I need, but how I'm going to pay for it. Because I'm not rich. I have nothing. But I'm the one with the information. Eddie can't use any tips I don't give him. When he bets on the sports details I feed him, he's going to be placing bets for me too. That's how I'm going to make the money I need. Betting on sports."

"So you're going to give insider info about the future to Eddie, something you swore you'd never do, to get rich? That's pretty damn shallow."

"Shallow? Trying to save the human race? You've got to be kidding me. I already promised you I'm not going to steal anymore. If I can't use Eddie to get me the money I need, what am I supposed to buy supplies with, my charm? I think we both know I don't have enough of that."

"I'll get a job. You can too."

Rosie laughs. It's so rare that she laughs that usually it sounds like music to me, but not this time.

"There's no way a job could pay enough money for the things I need to buy. How much do you think it costs to prepare for the end of the world? Millions, Carlos. I need millions of dollars, and right now we have" – she roots around in the bottom of her bag and withdraws a handful of crumpled bills – "seven bucks."

"Eddie can't make you millions of dollars, either."

"How do you know? With all the things I can predict, how do you know how much I can or can't make gambling?"

"Yeah, well, there's tons of bookies out there. I'm sure we can find a different one. We don't have to use Eddie's connections."

"I don't have time to find anybody else!" Rosie exclaims.

But there's a shadow hiding in her eyes. She's not telling me the whole truth, I'm sure of it. I bet she does have time to find someone else. She just doesn't want to. Right now it's easy. Eddie can do what she needs. If he happens to be the person who ruined my family, so be it. She doesn't care.

I press my lips together into a thin line. Part of me wants to get up and walk away; another part wants to yell at her until she understands what a jerk she's being. But I don't do either. It's as if all the warring feelings inside me repel each other like negatively charged magnets and send all the energy in my body funneling into my right leg, which is bouncing up and down like a gasoline-powered pogo stick.

I fold my arms across my chest and glare at the knee that won't stop moving so I don't have to look at Rosie. "You could come up with another plan if you wanted to," I mutter.

Rosie ignores me. And that bothers me more than anything else. Yesterday she welcomed my ideas. She relied on me. We planned things and made decisions together. Now I'm an annoyance. Someone trying to get in the way of her and her goal. A roadblock. It's like she flipped a switch and went from hot to cold instantly.

It reminds me of the time, not so long ago, when she first got her memories back. She didn't trust me enough to tell me about The Collapse. Instead, she charged all over Seattle vandalizing pretty much everything in her path and expecting me to follow while being a jerk and refusing to explain herself because I "wouldn't understand."

I nearly left her. I was moments away from melting off into the crowd. But then she saved that little kid from falling off a balcony like she was filming a scene from Spider-Man or something, and I stayed. And we worked it out. But here we are, a few days later, and we're slipping right back down that same exact slope.

Why is she so insistent on hitching her star to Eddie's? Why can't she find someone else to place sports bets for her? It can't possibly be that hard. I don't understand why she can feed Eddie all sorts of information, but I can't tell my brother to be safely inside a tall building on April 19th.

Even though she's not rudely telling me I don't understand, in this scenario I honestly don't. No matter what she says, I doubt if I ever will. And this time, I'm not sure if I can live with that.

CHAPTER SEVENTEEN

July 7, 2018 – David Columbia

David turns into the alley and creeps about midway down. He knows exactly where the boys have stationed themselves as they lie in wait, but he cranes his neck around, playing dumb. He positions himself next to a dumpster, which may come in handy. He looks away from where the boys hide, barely keeping them in his peripheral vision. "I was told I could meet Jimmy Squint," he whispers loudly. "Is anybody here?"

A hoot of laughter rings out, meant to sound disdainful, David suspects. "So's I hear you been lookin' for Lita."

From the corner of his eye, David watches a boy rise from a crouch and walk into the glow of a weak streetlight. He stands there for a moment waiting as he's flanked by two sentries on either side. Terrible military positioning. David has multiple avenues of escape – not that he'll need to run from any of these people. David examines the guards' stances and notes their individual weaknesses before focusing in on the boy in the middle.

He's probably technically a man, but something in his bearing indicates the insecurity of a child.

His right eyelid hangs lower than his left and a scar runs across it, like it was ripped and then poorly stitched.

"You must be Jimmy Squint."

"I don't remember introducing myself, old man."

David smothers a scoff. "It was an educated guess."

David's attitude and words are incongruous with his non-threatening posture. Jimmy clearly senses something's off. He rubs his palms against the hips of his jeans and slides one hand in a back pocket.

Palming a weapon, obviously. David adds another mental note to his running threat analysis. These three are no match for him, though they are certainly sure of their own invincibility. They're probably quite threatening for 2018, but it's nothing compared to what David has dealt with in The Towers.

"Yes, your intelligence is correct. I'm looking for Lita," David says conversationally. "Your sources are accurate."

"Put your fancy words away, old man. This isn't a spelling bee."

David raises an eyebrow and turns a corner of his mouth down. "I'm in a hurry. So let's take care of issue number one, shall we?"

"What's that?" Jimmy sneers.

David sweeps his leg out, hooking Jimmy's first henchman around the ankles and taking him down to the ground. He chops him in the throat with one hand and pounds his temple with the other. Lightning fast, he shifts to his right and shoots his hand out, grabbing the wrist of the other enforcer and applying enough pressure to make his hand spring open. The knife he'd been holding clatters to the pavement. David shifts again and uses the beefy man's body weight against him, flipping him over. His head lands on the curb, his body sprawled in the street. David stomps on his neck with a sickening crunch.

David pulls a knife from his ankle scabbard and flings it after the fleeing Jimmy. The blade tumbles end over end before finding its mark, burying itself in Jimmy's hamstring.

Jimmy's right leg buckles and he goes down with a howl.

David strides over to where Jimmy rolls from side to side on the alley pavement, writhing and trying to reach around to grab the knife protruding from the back of his thigh.

David yanks it out and examines the tip. *Dammit. Another knife chipped. Must have hit bone.* Jimmy screams and David kicks him in the ribs. "Shut up."

"You killed him," Jimmy blubbers.

"Who, Thing Two?" David shrugs. "Yeah, probably. Don't try to pretend like you were planning to let me live." He sinks to his haunches and sticks his thumb in the hole in Jimmy's thigh and presses. "Tell me everything you know about Lita, or this pain becomes worse."

Jimmy arches his back convulsively as he whimpers and whines. "I ain't seen her since the beginning of July."

David presses harder and digs with his thumbnail. "This *is* the beginning of July."

"You know what I mean, man! I ain't seen her since, I dunno, July 1st or something."

David rotates his thumb a quarter turn. "Why don't you try to remember more precisely?"

"July 2nd, dammit! It was July 2nd."

"What do you remember about that meeting? What made it special? What sticks out in your mind?" David releases the pressure on Jimmy's thigh wound.

Jimmy takes a deep, shuddering breath, then speaks quickly. "I wanted her to back me up when I took a delivery of some product at Pier 19. I expected trouble and there's nobody better than Lita if shit's about to go down."

"And did she join you at Pier 19?"

"No. She said she was busy."

"Busy doing what?"

"I don't know."

David's thumb dives back into Jimmy's wound and he howls.

"I'm never gonna walk again, man. You gotta stop."

David counts the throbs of Jimmy's pulse and does some quick calculations, factoring in Jimmy's pain level. "Your mobility is not my concern," David says through gritted teeth. "You are lying to me. Tell the truth and maybe you won't need a walker if I decide to let you go."

Jimmy twists around and his eyes gleam and widen fractionally. David knows the look on his face. It's the 'You're about to get served" look all petty criminals get when they think they're going to pull a fast one. David sighs, then whips a knife from his ankle sheath. Staying in a crouch and pivoting on his toes, he raises his arm and swipes it in an arc. Jimmy's first enforcer drops with a thud. A whistling sound bursts from a nine-inch-long slash across his throat, but there is no dying scream. The man's head is nearly severed.

"Now that we've got that out of the way," David says calmly, wiping the front and back of his knife off on Jimmy's shirt and sheathing the weapon, "maybe you'd like to be more forthcoming?"

"Oh, shit, man, oh, shit." Jimmy blubbers and squeezes his eyes shut.

"Listen, Squint," David says quietly. "I've had just about enough of this. I've given you far more time than you deserve. I've killed both your bodyguards. I have no love for zeds, but I'm not here to murder my way across Seattle. I'm searching for someone, and right now you're my best lead. If you are of no use…" David fingers the ankle sheath. "Well, as you can probably surmise, your life isn't worth much to me."

"I don't know all the words you just used, but you're gonna kill me if I don't talk, yeah?"

"Yeah," David affirms.

Words spill out of Jimmy's mouth like wastewater from a busted pipe. "Lita said she'd been here a whole year waiting for July 3rd cause she had business to take care of and that I'd have to find somebody else to do my dirty work. She called me a coward and said I was flimsier than a moth carcass."

"She said what?" David's eyebrows spring up. Now that Jimmy's holding nothing back, his information is far more surprising than David thought it would be. "Is that a common phrase here? Flimsier than a moth carcass?"

Tears gather at the corners of Jimmy's eyes and one slips down the side of his nose. "Nobody never said nothing like that to me before. I wouldn't take that shit from nobody. But Lita, she's different. I'm...I'm scared of her."

"Now that has the ring of truth. Keep talking."

"I begged her to meet me at the pier, but she brushed me off. She said she was almost in position and she told me to get lost."

"Where were you?"

"Downtown."

David jabs his finger in Jimmy's wound again. "Did you forget our terms, Squint? Be more specific."

"Outside, on the corner of...shit, the corner of...I don't remember the street name. It's where that statue of the big fat guy is, near the cop shop."

David nods. Second and Madison. He knows the area. His mind spins as he adds up all the information Jimmy gave him and makes sense of it. That moth carcasses statement raised the hair on the back of his neck. That's not how people talk in 2018. It isn't a phrase people say. But it will be. David grew up hearing – and using – that insult. It's something someone from The Towers would say.

Is that why Ellen sent Safeco the warning? Did she find out that she wasn't the only chrononaut Safeco sent to target Rosie? There is no Lita in 2074. Who is she? And how did Ellen find out about her? Were they a team?

"I need to locate her," David says resolutely. "If you have nothing else for me…" David flexes his fingers and reaches for Jimmy's pale scrawny neck.

"I can find her," he exclaims just before David's fingers graze his skin.

David raises his eyebrow skeptically. "And I'm just learning about this now? I think not."

"I heard a rumor," Jimmy squeals. "She was lookin' for Carlos Alvarez. If we find him, maybe we find her. And I know where he is."

Carlos. Rosie's kidnapper. David's heart grows cold. "I know that name."

"Yeah, I been hearing a lot about him last day or so. Whispers that she's been lookin' for him. I woulda said earlier, but…"

"But you would prefer I dig all the muscle out of your thigh first?"

"Goddammit, man, ten minutes ago I was more scared of Lita than I was of you. Now you guys are about equal, and you're the one who's standing right in front of me."

"Now we're back to the truth." David reaches into an inner pocket of his jacket and pulls out a roll of tape and a squishy substance that looks like a wad of old gum. "You're going to help me find Lita and this Carlos," he says evenly. "And you are not going to slow me down. When we're done, I'll decide whether you live or die."

He shoves the gum into Jimmy's wound.

Jimmy wails but cuts himself off abruptly. "Hey, it don't hurt anymore. What was that?"

One of Safeco's many inventions. "Something I brought from home. I wouldn't normally share it with you, but your leg wound is serious, and I can't have you slowing me down."

Jimmy groans. "If you don't kill me, Lita will."

David hauls Jimmy to his feet. "That's a chance you'll have to take."

CHAPTER EIGHTEEN

July 7, 2018 – Rosie

I know Carlos is pissed at me. I mean, I'd have to be an idiot to think everything's okay. It's not like he's doing a lot to hide his irritation. Or what if he is? What if he's masking most of his feelings and what I'm seeing now is just what's leaking out around his tight control? If that's the case, he might just spontaneously combust.

We spend the last half of the ferry ride in near total silence, and when the chime bing-bongs and the recorded voice says, *"Now arriving Seattle. This is Seattle,"* Carlos just gets up and stalks toward the front of the boat, expecting me to follow, I guess. The way he's treating me, strangers probably don't know we're together. Are we together? Or are we merely two people traveling in close proximity to each other?

I sidle next to Carlos and wait as the ferry bumps up against the dock and the workers lower the pedestrian ramp. "Do you want to stay in the bunker tonight?" I ask tentatively. "It's closer."

Lines of tension appear at the corners of his mouth. "No. It's too soon. If that chick really was following us, she might still be lurking around. We should go back to the camp at Scriber Lake."

"Will they have a tent for us, though? You said we wouldn't be back until tomorrow at the earliest."

"We're not staying in the bunker, Rosie," Carlos snaps.

"I'm not trying to say we should," I shoot back. "I just wonder if Scriber Lake is the best option."

"What, you want to go sleep under the University overpass? That was so much better?"

"That's not what I'm saying, either, Carlos. Why are you putting words in my mouth?"

We cross the pedestrian ramp and walk on the outer edge of the ferry terminal. Carlos's strides are long and he makes no effort to adjust his pace for my shorter legs. I might have grown four inches recently, but I'm still eight inches shorter than he is, and I have to scurry to keep up.

The ferry dock's light concrete walkway gives way to the darker city street, and Carlos doesn't stop until he reaches the corner of First Avenue.

He hunches his shoulders and stuffs his hands in his pockets. "The Scriber Lake group is safer than any mix of people downtown. Nobody's on hard drugs. Downtown is choked with junkies. Jordan's group is no meth, no heroin. That's where I want to be."

"That's fine."

"'Cause we might be there a while, and I don't want to have to be watching your back and mine all the time."

"I *said* that's fine," I snap, my voice sharp. "And I'm perfectly capable of watching my own back, thank you very much."

"Says the girl who didn't even know we were being followed on the bus," Carlos replies sarcastically.

The pedestrian walk signal turns and Carlos crosses the street, heading up the hill.

"Why are you picking a fight with me about everything?" I brush my hair back from my face and adjust my backpack.

"I'm not. I'm just treating you the way you've treated me ever since you met Eddie."

"What's that supposed to mean?"

Carlos scoffs, as if my question is totally illegitimate. "Like what I think doesn't matter."

"That's ridiculous."

"Oh, is it?"

"I didn't treat you bad at your brother's apartment."

"So you admit you treated me like shit everywhere else?"

"God, Carlos, will you knock it off? I'm under too much stress for this."

Carlos rolls his neck and stretches it from side to side. "Oh, right, your stress. You know what? We all have stress. Every goddamn minute of my life is stressful, trying to figure out where I'm going to sleep at night or where my next meal is going to come from or whether I'm going to be able to take care of my brother when I need to or wondering if I'm going to get stabbed by some rando under a bridge. So I've been really understanding about your stress and it would be kind of nice, a breath of fresh air, maybe, if you would recognize mine for a single goddamn second."

"Carlos, you know what? I'm sorry I introduced me to Eddie. Do you hear that? I am. I'm sorry. I wish you hadn't. Because maybe by some miracle I would have found some other magical person who can satisfy all my people's immediate needs and I wouldn't need him. But you did introduce me, and that's on you." The walk sign is already lit to cross Third Avenue. We don't pause when we reach the corner – we stride into the street.

"All your people's needs?" Carlos says, his voice sarcastic. "All they need is an indoor garden and gambling winnings? Sounds like you're set. And you talk about being under so much stress." Carlos scoffs and walks over to the closest bus stop, where he stares at the schedule while I try not to scream or tear the sign-post out of the sidewalk and hurl it down the street.

I'm not going to tell Carlos about the weapons I plan to buy from Eddie. There's no way that conversation will go well, but I'm still furious. "It's way more than a fracking indoor garden, Carlos, and you know that. You're being a jerk."

"Takes one to know one."

"What are you, five years old? Listen to yourself." I might have said more, but a northbound bus pulls up and the doors open.

Stomping up the stairs I dig out my pitifully small wad of one-dollar bills and deposit both our fares in the money chute. I stuff my last two dollars in my front pocket.

I sit down in a seat close to the front, by the window, and wait for Carlos to flop angrily into the seat next to me, but he doesn't. Instead, he chooses the seat behind mine.

My eyes prickle and burn with tears. Tears I refuse to shed. In just over nine months, fresh water will be so precious all our tear ducts will dry up. I swallow hard and try not to choke on the bile rising in my throat. I ball my hands into fists and command my heart to harden. I imagine it drying up, crackling and shrinking in my chest, until all that's left is a crumpled, pockmarked lump. I've been a fool. I've changed since I've been here in the past. It's time to get back to the person I was when I came here. Because that's the person I need to be if I'm going to have any chance of saving humanity.

This is why Carlos isn't in any of the stories or legends about Rosarita. I'm sure of it. Tonight, right now, this is where he leaves me. Maybe in his mind, he already has.

When the bus drops us off in Lynnwood, we walk silently from the transit center to the park. Once we get to the campsite, he pokes his head into the tent we slept in last night, turns to me and says, "It's still ours," and crawls inside. It's the first time he's spoken to me since we got off the bus.

Instead of crawling in after him, I go to the girls' bathroom area in the woods. After I do my business, I stare up at the sky for a long time. I want to see stars, but they've never revealed themselves to me. You can't see them through the radioactive haze where I'm from. During all my previous trips to the past, I stayed in the city, where the ambient light is too bright to see them. Even here, in the woods, the light from the suburbs spills into the sky from all around, masking anything I might see otherwise. I'm starting to wonder if they're even real. Carlos said they were. He said he'd show them to me. He also said I was his girl. And I'm pretty sure he lied about that, so what's to stop him from lying about stars too? I wouldn't know any better.

In nine months, even if I want to cry, I won't be hydrated enough. I might as well give into my feelings now while I can. I place my palms and forehead against a tree trunk and I cry.

When I've exhausted every tear in my body, I stumble my way back to the campsite and crawl into the tent I shared with Carlos last night. What a difference a day makes. Last night we cuddled, happy and – I thought – in love. I should have known better. My future is bound up in duty and sacrifice. Happiness and romance are not for me.

Carlos is a lump in the darkness, turned toward the canvas wall of the tent. Just when I decide he must be asleep, he speaks. "I thought you weren't coming back."

There are so many things I could say right now and maybe start to fix things, but the phrase that slips out of my mouth seems placed there by an evil witch, determined to ruin my future. "Sorry to disappoint you," I say.

"Go to sleep, Rosie."

I chew on the inside of my cheek and flop down next to him, rolling away so that our backs are to each other. I pull a thin blanket over myself and hear his last words echo in my brain. *"Go to sleep, Rosie."* I'd love to. But I have a feeling it's going to be a long time before rest comes.

CHAPTER NINETEEN

July 8, 2018 – Rosie

I haven't slept so poorly since I left The Towers. When I first arrived in 2018, I had no memories, so I didn't have anything to keep me awake all night worrying. Then I was really sick and medicated to sleep most nights. After that, I had Carlos to hold me. On those nights, the only thing that kept me up was his kisses, and I had no complaints about that. But I'm in insomnia's grip now, and it's definitely not due to being overly kissed. My stupid thoughts churn relentlessly and won't leave me alone.

If I give up my Eddie connection, my people will all die. Either of starvation or violence. It seems counterintuitive that the guns I buy from Eddie will protect my people, but it's the truth. In the early days, insurrection will be common as people go tribal, but I know I persevere, and it's not because I'm so rational and knowledgeable. It's because I'm the one with the weapons and ammo. My guns keep the peace.

So what changes? my brain whispers. *Do those guns still keep the peace? Or do they keep people in their places, held down and submissive?*

I shake my head. Rosarita died more than sixteen years before I was born. I can't blame her for everything that's gone wrong since then. My eyes pop open. Oh my god. I know when I die. I'll be logged as lost on July 8th, 2057. I stare into the darkness, counting up from the Fourth of July. Today is July 8th. It's the anniversary of my death... thirty-nine years from now. I'll be fifty-five years old when I die. And I basically already know how my whole life is going to go. I'm Rosarita Columbia, the woman who prepared for the unthinkable and saved humanity. I have a son, David, who I raise to lead. I have no love story. No romance. No Carlos.

I must drop into a coma-like sleep some time long after dawn because I jerk awake at the sounds of people rustling around the campsite, talking in low tones.

I rub my bleary eyes and twist around under the blankets. Carlos is already gone. He left the tent, and I slept right through it. Shaking the blankets off me, I struggle to a sitting position, then get to my hands and knees and crawl out of the tent. Is that it? Is he gone for good?

No, there he is, sitting across the campground on a fallen log, sipping on something out of a dull metal cup. He gazes at me over the rim of his mug, like he's been watching our tent flap all morning, just waiting for this moment. I try to smile at him, but my mouth is trembling so hard, I'm not sure if I'm able to curl my lips up enough for him to even tell that I'm making the effort.

He takes a last sip and dumps his drink out on the ground behind him. He doesn't smile back at me, and whatever expression I did manage to paste onto my face slides right off. I rise to my feet and cross to the log he sits at, taking a spot a couple feet away from him.

"Do you have any more of whatever you were drinking?" I

ask. My voice is scratchy and sounds weirder than normal to my ears.

"It'll be in that pot over there if there's anything left," Carlos says, waving casually toward a kettle strung over smoldering coals.

If his voice were any cooler, I'd be able to see his breath hanging in the air, and I feel my heart shrivel another millimeter. But I cross to the kettle to get myself a drink. Just before I grab it with my bare hand, Carlos barks a warning. "Use a hot pad."

Shep, one of the guys who lives here too, hands me a tattered but thick brown pad, and I wrap it around the handle. Even with the protection, I can feel the heat of the kettle through the pad, and I shoot Carlos a grateful look. I would have burned myself badly without his warning. How far we've fallen, that in the course of one day I can go from being his special girl to being contented by the fact that he didn't let me burn myself. I guess I'll take what I can get.

"Where's Jordan?" I ask of no one in particular.

Shep clears his throat. "Jordan has a new friend. I don't know when they plan to come up for air."

Oh. Well, good for her. Maybe there's a limited amount of happiness available in the world and Carlos and I had to fall out of love in order for Jordan to receive that kind of joy. I don't honestly believe that's the way things work, but the thought still makes me feel morose.

"I didn't expect to see you two until later today at the earliest," Shep says to Carlos. Shep's head bobs rhythmically, like one of the pigeons downtown. It's as though he's pecking at something invisible just a few inches in front of him. I'm used to nervous tics in The Towers, but it's still hard to look away from because you don't see nearly as much of that kind of stuff in 2018 as you do in my time.

"Yeah, well, we finished our business over in Bremerton and we wanted to get back."

Shep incorporates a nod into his head bob. I settle on the log again and take a sip of my beverage. It's coffee, weak but very hot. I'll miss hot drinks after The Collapse. I wish there were some way we could warm drinks without fire, it's so comforting, but of course there's not. And fire's been outlawed in The Towers for decades. Too dangerous.

I take another long swig and savor the scalding feeling in my throat, knowing that sensation is doomed for extinction. There won't be unlimited opportunities for this kind of simple pleasure. This and all sorts of other little moments of joy are numbered.

Across the clearing, in the tent next to mine and Carlos's, I hear laughter and soft voices. The canvas side of the tent shakes a little, like someone is rolling around or wrestling in there, then Jordan's dark head of hair pokes out. She has a smile on her face a mile wide, her gold front tooth shining like the sun.

She catches sight of me, but as she opens her mouth in greeting, she lets out a squeal as she's yanked back inside the tent, the top of her head disappearing behind the flaps. "Lemme go," Jordan squeals.

"Never. I'm keeping you," someone else growls playfully. I have a flash of homesickness. One of the only good things about 2074 is my letter-mate, Ellen, and that sounded just like her.

I wrap my arms around myself and tremble. I have to get out of here. Carlos doesn't want a truce and these are his people, not mine. I'll be fine on my own in Seattle while I prepare for The Collapse. I can survive better than any of these street people. I have tricks up my sleeve they can't even imagine. I know I'll succeed because I still have all my knowledge of the future and it's intact and unchanged. I somehow thought I would have help. But I must not. I mean, I know I'll use Eddie to get money and guns and to get the hydroponics set up, but that's not the same thing as having a team. None of the legends indicate that I had anybody by my side. I guess the more deeply I fell in love with Carlos, the more I assumed I would have a support system.

I stand up abruptly. "I'm going for a walk." Because I'm a glutton for punishment, I give Carlos one last chance. "Do you want to come with me?"

Carlos shakes his head. "I need another cup of coffee. I slept like shit."

I can't say anything because even though I know I have another thirty-nine years ahead of me, I just died inside. I issue a sharp nod, turn on my heel, and walk into the woods. I don't look back.

CHAPTER TWENTY

July 8, 2018 – Carlos

I watch Rosie walk into the woods and I want to call out to her, but the angry animal inside of me holds my tongue in a vise grip. I need a little time to cool off. We probably both do. When she comes back, we'll go somewhere to find some lunch and we'll talk it out. In the light of day, with Eddie miles behind us and food in our stomachs, we'll both feel better. We'll work it out.

Jordan's tent walls shake like they're being buffeted by hurricane-force winds and screams of laughter emanate from inside. At least someone's having fun. The tent flap flies back and Jordan crawls out again. This time nobody grabs her and yanks her backward. Instead, she's followed by another occupant. When I register who it is, my mouth drops open. Our eyes meet, and her jaw goes slack too, mirroring mine.

"Shit, Jordan," I bark, scrambling to my feet, "that's the chick who was stalking me in Seattle. It's Lita! What is she doing here? I thought you had standards."

Jordan blanches, but Lita stands stoically, her head thrown

back, absorbing my words. Jordan clears her throat. She doesn't look happy or playful anymore. Instead, her features are wary, and she speaks carefully to me. "When she arrived in camp, I knew her as Lita. But she's proven herself an asset, and she told us yesterday she prefers to go by the name 'Ellen' now." She reaches to her side and takes Lita's hand and they lace their fingers together.

I feel like my eyes are so wide that they're going to fall out of my head, plop plop on the forest floor. "Going by a new name doesn't make her a good person, Jordan. Are you out of your mind? I get that you guys are having a good time and whatever, but she's dangerous and no name change is going to fix that. She's one of Jimmy Squint's enforcers. She lives in The Jungle. She's into all sorts of shit you want nothing to do with. Crap, Jordan, they say she killed a guy."

Jordan raises her chin. "I've heard the stories. But events of the past day have convinced me otherwise. If you want to stay here at Scriber Lake, with us, you'll have to accept her."

I can't believe what I'm hearing. "We've known each other a long time, Jordan, and 'irrational' has never been a word I'd use to describe you, but come on! This chick stalked me in north Seattle. She's the reason I left, for god's sake!"

Jordan tilts her head at Lita. "Did you?"

Lita nods. "I didn't mean to scare you or run you off. I had a business proposition for you. It's okay now. I don't need you anymore. I got it covered."

"If you don't need me anymore, then why are you here? Did you follow me up here?"

"No, she—" Jordan starts, but Lita quiets her with a hand on her arm.

"I'll go now."

"Ellen, you don't have to go and I don't want you to. I'm the leader of this camp. If anyone has to leave, it's Carlos and Rosie. After she gets her medicine, of course."

Medicine? What is Jordan talking about?

Jordan looks around the clearing. "Where's your girl? Where's Rosie?" she asks.

I purse my lips. "She went for a walk."

"She doesn't know these woods, does she?"

"Nah, but she'll be fine. She's resourceful," I say tersely.

"It's okay, baby," Lita, or Ellen, or whatever her name is, says to Jordan. "We need breakfast anyway. Walk me to the path."

I narrow my eyes as they walk away. Jordan throws a scathing look over her shoulder at me. She can be as pissed as she wants; she's the one who's harboring a criminal in her supposedly safe-space camp. The one person I'm not worried about in this scenario is Rosie. I've seen her in action enough times to know that Lita's no match for her. If they come up against each other in the woods and there's a scrap, I might even pity Lita. I watch her duck to enter the path, pulling poor starstruck Jordan behind her. Nah, whatever might happen to Lita, I'm sure she more than deserves it.

CHAPTER TWENTY-ONE

July 8, 2018 – Ellen

I tug on Jordan's hand and we enter the woods together. I'm trembling, but it's not with anticipation, even though I'm about to save Rosie. President David Columbia, my new uncle, is counting on me. When I deliver his daughter to him, my safety, comfort, and position will be ensured for the rest of my life. And even if that reward wasn't spilled out in front of me like a yellow brick road, I'd do it anyway, because I love Rosie. But I'm not excited about it at all. My fingertips tighten around Jordan's and I realize why. Yes, I love Rosie, but I'm not in love with her after all. I didn't really know what falling in love felt like until it hit me like a twenty-foot wave.

I have to leave Jordan now. But I will never, ever forget her. When I curl up on my cot in The Towers at night, clutching at nothing, it will be her body I imagine lying beside me, her face burned into the inside of my eyelids.

I push through the bushes, linked to Jordan, until I come to a spot where we can both stand. I won't be on this path long, but she doesn't know that. "I need to go look for my cousin," I say haltingly. "I'm worried she'll have another seizure out there in the woods. Carlos doesn't know her as well as I do."

Jordan nods, clear-eyed and trusting. Can I kiss her one more time without losing myself forever? I have to try. I twist one of her loose curls around my fingertip gently and pull her close for the sweetest, most heartbreaking kiss of my life. My eyes burn and I pull back quickly, swiping the back of my hand across my eyes before she can see my pain. I feel like my heart is ripping in half. The most vibrant, colorful person I've ever known is a zed, and I'm not simply leaving her, I'm leaving her to die.

"Jordan," I say quickly before I lose my nerve, "you gotta promise me something."

Jordan licks her lips and gives me a smile. "Okay, I'd say you've earned one promise."

I take two steps back from her so that I'm not tempted to touch her again. "Do you swear you'll do what I ask?"

She wrinkles her brow prettily, but she nods. "I promise."

"Okay then. On the morning of April 19th, you have get to the highest floor of the tallest building you can find and you have to stay there all day."

Jordan's smile slips. "Um, that's kind of random."

"You promised," I say. "Don't you dare forget. April 19th." My heart hammers in my chest, a panicked double-time beat. I whirl and dive into a hole in the bushes, scrambling on my hands and knees until I reach the first big tree I come to. I climb quickly, hand over hand, pulling myself up until I'm twenty feet in the air. Below me, I see Jordan on the path. "Ellen?" she calls, looking around. "When are you coming back?"

But I don't answer. Because I can't bear to force the horrid words out through my voice box.

Never. I'm never coming back.

I have to get away from here. The trees are so thick and dense that I leap lightly from branch to branch, putting distance between myself and Jordan far faster than I could on the ground.

From up here, I canvass the forest floor as easily as if I were skipping down a sidewalk. Not that I'd ever skip.

With my high-up vantage point, I realize there are more people hidden in the forest than I knew. In a clump of bushes, a couple sleeps half-naked and entwined around each other. Farther on, a woman slumps against the base of a tree. Is that Rosie? I can't see her face. I pause and watch her for a moment. She turns and vomits into her own lap. A needle dangles uselessly out of the crook of her arm. No, that's not her. This woman's skin is stretched too tightly over high, unfamiliar cheekbones. I move on, leaping from branch to branch making no more noise than the squirrels I repeatedly startle.

Did I blunder off in the wrong direction? Did Rosie double back to rejoin Carlos? I'm afraid I missed my chance. Then I hear the tiniest of sounds. It reminds me of the mewling of a sack of life I found abandoned in the city one night when I first arrived here. Jimmy threw the whole bag of creatures off an overpass. I found out later they were called "kittens."

The sound is coming from a girl huddled at the base of the tree I'm standing in. My heart leaps in my chest. It's Rosie, and she's sobbing her eyes out.

I never had a solid plan for how I would reveal myself to Rosie when I found her. Based on her attachment to Carlos, I've always assumed I'd probably need to take her by surprise. Most likely I'd knock her out and drag her unconscious body to the city. It might take her a couple days to fall out from under Carlos's spell. But I knew she would thank me later.

Now I look back at that naïve, stupid girl I was just twenty-four hours ago. Rosie loves Carlos. She would never thank me for ripping her away from him against her will. If I did that, she'd do everything in her power to return to him. It would be the worst way to try to recover her.

No, I can't take her by force. Rosie must know as well as I do that she can't stay here, that she has to leave him to his fate. But like me, it's killing her. I want to cry like Rosie is, but I can't. Not now, not yet. I have a mission to complete.

Rosie and I are both going to leave pieces of ourselves here in the past, pieces neither one of us will ever be able to recover. Our hearts will always beat with the same relentless pain, and it will bring us closer together than ever. But I get it now. She has to come to this decision on her own. She must choose to leave. She's not stupid. She'll know going home is the only real option, but she has to have time and space to grieve. I'm not going to trick Rosie or stun her into submission. I will be honest. I will do this right.

I crouch on the branch, grab it with both hands, then allow my body to dangle in the air, my toes five feet above where Rosie shudders, her body wracked by one silent, convulsive sob after another. Letting go of the branch, I drop to the forest floor.

CHAPTER TWENTY-TWO

July 8, 2018 – Rosie

I hear the soft thud of something falling out of the tree above me, and I have the craziest flash of homesickness. The noise is like the sound our body makes in stairwell jump training when we clear a landing successfully.

I'm so wrapped up in my thoughts of home that I literally visualize Ellen crouched in front of me, reaching toward me, her fingertips tentative and trembling. Well, this is it. I've snapped and completely lost my sanity. My mind, in an effort to shield me from my own pain and sorrow, has created an apparition of my letter-mate to console me. *Nice try, brain, but now I'm just that much crazier.*

"Rosie?" the mirage in front of me says.

I blink back at her, each fluttering of my lashes beating another couple of drops out of my waterlogged eyes. Now she's talking to me? A side trip down Delusion Alley might have been nice, but it's probably not a good idea to humor my damaged brain on this one.

I squeeze my eyes shut tightly and open them again. She's still there.

I scrounge a handful of pine needles off the forest floor and fling them at her, expecting them to pass through her spectral body, which will then dissipate in a haze.

Instead, they hit her, and she looks at herself in surprise. Most of the needles fall off, but she brushes a few strays that try to stick to her and gives me a very concerned look. "Rosie? Is there something wrong? Don't you remember me?"

Slowly, she reaches toward me, like she's afraid I'm the one who's going to disappear in a puff of smoke. But when her fingertips find my arm, her spectral hand doesn't pass right through me. Instead, I feel her warm fingers press against my wrist.

"Ellen?" I whisper.

"God, it's good to hear my name. I thought you might not remember me, and then for a second, I thought you were going to call me 'Lita' like everyone else does when they first see me," she says, tears spilling from her eyes. I've never seen Ellen cry before, and that's when I'm convinced that she's real. There's no way my brain would concoct a vision of Ellen crying.

Ellen. My replacement letter-mate after I lost Rachel. My life's partner. She'd die for me, and in a way, she already has. Because here she is, scant months before The Collapse, when everyone perishes. That can't be a coincidence. All these thoughts crash through my head as we throw ourselves into each other's arms. We're both making keening, nonsensical sounds. I stroke Ellen's hair. It's long and healthy, just like mine. "Ellen," I whisper. "You're really here."

"I found you," she whispers back.

It feels like eons have passed, but really, it's only been a few seconds. She takes both my hands in hers, kneels in front of me, and squeezes. "Let's go home."

CHAPTER TWENTY-THREE

July 8, 2018 – Carlos

Jordan sits next to me on the fallen log, her chin in her hand, staring at the teakettle swinging over the dead fire. She's been that way ever since she came back from the woods without Lita.

"Rosie's been gone a long time," I say to break the silence.

"Maybe Ellen found her," Jordan replies.

"Don't say that." I groan.

"Why? That's why she came here."

I rocket to standing so fast, I practically levitate for a second. "Lita was following me. For Jimmy. She said so." My words are coming out too fast, and there's a panicked note in my voice.

"I don't know why she said that. I mean, maybe Jimmy did want you for something, but she came here to find Rosie. She's her cousin."

"Rosie doesn't have a cousin."

"How do you know that?"

"I just know. She has a dad, but no other family."

"Well, you're wrong," Jordan says matter-of-factly. "Ellen's her older cousin. Didn't you notice how much they look alike? Ellen's been looking for her. She has her medicine and she's been really worried."

"Her medicine?"

"Yeah. For Rosie's seizures."

"Rosie doesn't have seizures."

"Um, Carlos, I saw her have one with my own two eyes. She was right over there." Jordan points across the campground to the other side of the fire, where Rosie and I had been snuggled when a discussion about spiders caused Rosie to convulse and grow four inches instantaneously. But Jordan doesn't know what really caused that episode. She has no idea that Rosie is a time traveler, and that the spider conversation changed the future world so significantly that Rosie's entire body grew, changed, and filled out. And I can't tell Jordan that. She'd never believe me.

"That was a one-time thing," I say tightly. My heart hammers in my chest. Something is very, very wrong about all of this.

"Ellen has been looking for her for ages, trying to get Rosie's medicine to her, and she followed her to this camp. She was really upset when she found out that she just missed her." Jordan's lips part and her eyes drift up and to the right, the classic pose of someone scanning through their own memories. "But we worked it out."

My head feels like it's spinning. Rosie doesn't have seizures. She doesn't have a cousin. Everyone she knows hasn't even been born yet. "None of this makes any sense."

Jordan sighs heavily. "It took us a few minutes to get everything sorted out with Ellen, but once we did and she decided to stay, she proved her worth. She's a great person. I know you don't want to believe that, but we've all done some shit to stay alive. None of us are saints."

"It doesn't add up. And you might just have to trust me on this, Jordan, but you've known me a long time and you know I'm not a liar. Rosie doesn't have a cousin. And she doesn't have seizures. There is no medicine. Lita—"

"Ellen," Jordan says, cutting me off sharply.

I roll my eyes and huff. "Ellen," I say, over-enunciating the name, "made that shit up. Dammit. This is bad."

Jordan sighs again. "I know you don't like her, but I do. Unfortunately, I kind of got the feeling that she was blowing me off when she left. I'm not sure she's coming back."

Ellen, or Lita, or whatever her name is, is out there in the forest looking for Rosie on a made-up pretense, and now Jordan tells me this? I know that Rosie can handle anything that chick might throw at her and probably laugh in her face while mopping the forest floor with her, but I'm still totally on edge. "What did she say that made you think she was gone for good?"

Jordan shakes her head as if she's being bothered by a gnat and brushes her curls back from her face. "It was just super random and weird. So she's all, 'Promise me something,' and I'm like, 'Okay' and I thought she was gonna say something silly or sexy like, 'Don't wear underwear today' or something, but she was all, 'Get to the highest building you can on April 19th and stay there all day.'" She lets her chin flop back into her hand and stares at me glumly.

"She said what?" I whisper, my voice barely squeezing past the muscles of my throat, which have constricted to the width of a needle.

"I know. What a weird way to blow somebody off. And seriously? Like, I'm supposed to hang out at the Lynnwood Convention Center all day or something? Why?"

"That's not what she meant," I say, my voice still strangled. "She meant Seattle."

"How do you know?"

"Because she knows. She knows about The Collapse." The weight of my statement and everything it means hits me like a bucket of ice cold water. Lita's a killer from the future. She's not here for me. She was following us, but it's never been about me. She's after Rosie, and she's out there, right now, stalking her in the woods. And Rosie has no idea.

My throat unclenches, I take a huge breath, and I bellow. "Rosie! Boo!" I don't even attempt to hunker down to get on the path. I crash straight through the bushes like an enraged bear. She's out there all alone, and I love her. I must find her before Lita does. Rosie's life depends on it.

CHAPTER TWENTY-FOUR

July 8, 2018 – David Columbia

"Which way, Squint?"

"I dunno for sure. This isn't my turf, man."

David stifles a sigh of exasperation. If it isn't Jimmy's turf, it certainly isn't his own. He's never been north of the city before. Business has taken him to Tacoma on a few occasions and Bellevue once, but everything north of the bunker is a black hole to David.

In another time, he'd be intrigued by the potential and the possibilities that Everett, the next big city to the north, might hold, but right now he has no bandwidth for anything other than finding Rosie and the bastard Carlos who took her. He's used to multitasking and handling multiple priorities at once, but in this case he is laser-focused on a single outcome: retrieving Rosie. He's so close, he can almost sense her presence. This is it. He's certain of it.

"Lemme go check a map," Jimmy says.

"Not so fast, Squint. I'm coming with you."

Jimmy sighs. "Man, I know you can throw a knife. You really think I'd try to take off on you?"

David shrugs. "Yes, I do. You don't strike me as particularly intelligent."

Jimmy grinds his teeth together so hard, David hears the molars ratcheting against each other. They walk to a posted map and Jimmy and David both scan it. "Crap," Jimmy says. "This is just a route map. Scriber Lake's not on here." He looks east and west. "So it could be either that way, or that way," he says, pointing each direction in turn. He looks north. "Or that way." He pivots south and his mouth drops open.

"Or that way," David says sarcastically. "Yes, I get it."

"Nah, man," Jimmy breathes, his voice barely above a whisper. "We don't need to find the park."

David wrinkles his eyebrows together. "Why not?"

"Lita, man," Jimmy says, his voice growing stronger. "She's on that goddamn bus right over there."

David's eyes follow Jimmy's flailing hand to the southeastern-most bus bay. And there she is, her profile unmistakable in the window seat of the bus. And it can't possibly be Lita. Because it's Ellen.

"Do you see her, man? She's right over there. In the bus that's leaving right now."

That statement unlocks all of David's frozen muscles. "It's what?"

As if on cue, the bus shudders and belches smoke, then lurches away from the curb. David turns on his afterburners and sprints after the bus, but it's too late. It swings a wide right turn and enters a carpool-only mass transit lane to merge onto the southbound freeway.

"Frack!" David screams.

To his credit, Jimmy doesn't try to run. He's standing stock still where David left him. With long, angry steps, David eats up the distance between them. "That woman's name is Ellen! But I know her, and I'm looking for her too. She's a better lead than Lita. Why didn't you see her five seconds earlier?"

Jimmy quakes.

"Where is that bus going?" David asks.

"It was a 512. So downtown. The next one comes in fifteen minutes."

David closes his eyes briefly and takes a deep breath through his nose. I don't have fifteen minutes." He reaches into an inner pocket of his jacket and withdraws a hammer.

"How many weapons do you have hidden on you, man?" Jimmy cries.

David ignores him and strides over to a dark brown older model Buick in the parking lot. He rears back and smashes the passenger side window, reaches inside, and pulls up on the interior door handle. "Get in."

CHAPTER TWENTY-FIVE

July 8, 2018 – Ellen

I'd thought that it might be hard to convince Rosie to leave the park with me, but a broken heart is a powerful agent of change.

I didn't realize when I saw her crying in the forest that it was because her relationship with Carlos had just ended. I didn't know they'd broken up. I thought she was feeling like I was – devastated that she couldn't save the one she loved. Now I can't decide who I feel sorrier for, her or me. I mean, Carlos knows about The Collapse and he chose certain death over her. That's devastating. But walking away from Jordan might feel even worse because *I* chose it. I think I'd rather be in Rosie's position, which is weird because the last thing I've ever wanted to be is a victim.

Now Rosie and I sit side by side on the bus, waiting for it to pull out of the bay and take us back to Seattle. "I think once we get back to our own time and have some space and distance, we'll feel better," I say, but I don't believe my own words. I'll never feel better about leaving Jordan. I know what's waiting for me in The

Towers. I feel like this was my one shot at happiness. If it weren't for my deep love for Rosie and my commitment to her, I would have chosen facing The Collapse with Jordan by my side, no question about it. It amazes me that I think that way after Rosie's dad offered me a familial tie and made me his niece. My position in The Towers is assured as soon as we return. But I've fallen in love, and that's a wildcard I never expected.

"I thought I had it all figured out. I had some really wild ideas," Rosie says, her voice quavering. "But I must have been wrong if we're really going home."

I know she must mean spending her life with Carlos. And I get it. I had wild ideas too, about Jordan. I'm sure Rosie and I will always imagine the lives we would have led with these zeds who captured our hearts if The Collapse wasn't our reality. But we'll have to be content with daydreams.

Rosie's next words seem to parallel my thoughts and help give them shape. "I always assumed people just sort of eased into love. Like, you'd know someone for a long time and you'd slowly figure out that you love them. But that's not the way it works."

"Maybe that's how love is in our time. Here in the past, love seems so easy, doesn't it? Like everything just *has* to work out. But it won't. We know better than that."

Rosie raises a knee to her chest, balls her fist, and rests her chin on it. "The things I thought I had figured out can't possibly be true now that you've rescued me. I don't know. I'm so mixed up. Nothing makes sense to me anymore. Do you think maybe fate sent us here to learn how to love?"

No. General Safeco sent me here to kill you. Fate had nothing to do with that. But I can't say that. Not now. I'll have to tell Rosie sometime, but right now, it's more productive to just agree with her. I nod, and it occurs to me that maybe on some weird meta-physical plane, Rosie speaks the truth. "I was only with Jordan for twenty-four hours," I say quietly, "but it changed me forever."

"I really liked her," Rosie agrees, sniffling.

It pains me that we're already talking about her as if she's dead and gone. The bus pulls away from the curb and motors toward the freeway.

"I wish we could plunge from up here in Lynnwood and just get it over with," Rosie says. "But there'd be no way to get back to The Towers once we arrived in our own time. Everything up here is underwater."

I haven't talked through the logistics of getting home at all. Rosie assumes I have the chemicals we'll need. But I don't. All I have is one set of chemicals General Safeco gave me when I first left on this mission, and nobody knows about those. Uncle David, Rosie's father, has sets of chemicals for all three of us.

Again, Rosie speaks as if she's reading my mind and picking up on my train of thought. "You know I was going to bring Carlos back with me? I mean, I was going to try at least."

My breath catches in surprise. "Can you do that?"

Rosie shrugs. "I don't see why not. When I left a note for my dad in Smith Tower, I asked him to bring three sets of return chemicals with him. One for him, one for me, and one for Carlos, but I just said the third set was for my friend." Her brow wrinkles and she turns her body on the seat to face me more fully. "Did he get my message? How many sets of return chemicals did he send you with?"

I shake my head. Uncle David didn't get Rosie's message because I was following the traitor Safeco's orders and I destroyed the communication box and everything inside it. Should I tell her that now? No. Not yet. She needs to know everything, but I'll tell her the whole story once we're all back in 2074. We'll deal with Safeco and his treachery together, all three of us. "Your dad never got your note. He only knew you were alive when he got the message you left in Columbia Tower."

Rosie tilts her head and gives me a confused look. "I didn't leave a message in Columbia Tower."

"'Help me Daddy?' Written in black marker on the mural? I saw it myself. Are you saying that wasn't you?"

Rosie's eyes widen and she gasps. "That *was* me! When I first arrived here my mind was a total blank and I didn't have any memories, but certain things really scared me. Water. Going downhill. Me and Carlos were up in Columbia using the bathroom and somebody said the word 'collapse' and I freaked out. I didn't really even know what I was doing, but I scribbled that in the corner of the mural. Carlos was so mad."

I curl my arm around Rosie's shoulders and hug her to my side. "For weeks, your dad thought you were dead, then that message showed up."

"And he sent you to bring me back."

I wince and clench my jaw. "Not exactly. But we're working together now," I finish in a rush.

Rosie chews on her lips. "There's a lot you're not telling me, isn't there?"

She's nobody's fool. I nod. "Yeah. Honestly, there is. But I think it's better if we wait to go into it until we're back home."

Rosie nods. "Okay."

That's the thing about letter-mates. We don't have to waste our time convincing each other that we're doing what's best. Even letter-mates that don't like each other personally would die for each other. It's our world.

Rosie takes a deep, shuddering breath. "So Dad doesn't know I wanted three sets of return chemicals. I really am leaving Carlos behind."

I sniff disdainfully. "Rosie, based on what you told me, he made that decision himself."

Rosie shrugs one shoulder. "I thought he loved me. And maybe he did. But I guess he stopped."

"You don't just stop loving people, Rosie. I know I'm new to this too, but I'm sure I'm right about that. Maybe sometimes love's not enough."

"It should be. I think it's more likely that he never loved me at all."

"No, I think he did," I say absentmindedly. My thoughts have veered to Jordan. Would love be enough for us if I were to stay here?

Rosie's reply is sharp. "How would you know? You never even met him," she says.

Frack. I've painted myself into a corner, and I'm not quite sure how to extricate myself from where this conversation will inevitably lead. "Um, actually, that's not technically true."

Rosie shifts in her seat and spears me with a look. "What are you keeping from me, Ellen?"

The only way I can think of to answer her question is with one of my own. "How long have you been here, Rosie?" I ask carefully.

"Since the middle of June."

That's it? Wow. Safeco sent me way out in advance of her arrival. I try not to let the surprise show on my face. "I've been here, uh, quite a bit longer than that. Looking for you. I met Carlos before you arrived. And, um, I saw you guys together. It took me some time to find a good moment to approach you."

Rosie is quiet for just a second and I think I might have given her a satisfactory answer, but then she explodes. "A good moment? Frack, Ellen, we are nine months away from The Collapse. I've been going out of my mind. I thought I was lost here forever. I was legitimately planning how I was going to survive the whole thing and bring humanity through the darkness with me. I thought I was some kind of savior. And it was all for nothing."

The bus must go over a bump because I jolt oddly in my seat. Rosie gets a weird surprised expression on her face. She reaches out and pokes me hard in the abdomen.

"Hey," I exclaim.

"Sorry," she mutters, "I just...never mind." She shakes her head as if to clear it. "You know what?" she says. "I can't have this conversation on a bus in 2018. Let's talk about this when we get back. But I don't want to do it on the comm. We're going straight to my quarters and you're going to tell me everything. Every. Fracking. Thing."

I nod firmly. "Absolutely."

Rosie falls silent and stares at her folded hands in her lap for a while. I don't know where her mind has gone, but she twists her fingers relentlessly, as if she's lost in thought. The bus slows in traffic and that seems to jar her back to reality. "So, I guess we go to Columbia and plunge from the twenty-first floor as per our typical protocol?"

Here we go. "Um, it's actually not that simple."

"What's the wrinkle?"

I swallow hard. My throat is as dry as sandpaper. "I don't have the return chemicals."

Rosie's mouth drops open. "What?" she whispers. "How is that even possible?"

I blink rapidly. "It's all tied up in the weird story of how I got here in the first place, and I swear I'll explain everything to you once we're home."

"How are we going to get home without return chemicals?" Rosie's voice rises almost hysterically. I know she's been through a lot, but so have I. Maybe even more. She lost her love. I threw mine away.

"We'll get them," I say, an edge to my voice.

"How?" Rosie cries, ignoring my warning tone. "I don't know the formula. I always went with a return set of chemicals in my vest. I had to use that set to get here in the first place. It was the only way I could escape drowning. Oh my god," Rosie breathes, her voice full of wonderous dread. "Now it makes sense. That's why nothing's changed. Because nothing *has* changed. And nothing will. I'm still stuck here. We're not going anywhere. The Collapse is still going to happen to us."

"No, it won't," I assure her.

Rosie drops her face into her hands.

"It won't happen," I say in my strongest, most confident voice. "Because we're meeting your dad at Columbia. He has our return chemicals."

"Daddy?" Rosie turns her head and looks all over the bus, as if I said he was in the seat behind us rather than at Columbia Tower. "My dad is here in 2018?"

I hope that any of the panic I feel isn't showing on my face. I gave David an excellent clue about where I'd meet him once I found Rosie. But did he figure it out? And more than that, did he trust me? Will he be there waiting for us in Columbia Tower? My heart tells me *yes*. But I honestly don't know for sure.

I grip Rosie's hands tightly in my own. "Absolutely," I say firmly. "He's there waiting for us right now."

CHAPTER TWENTY-SIX

July 8, 2018 – David Columbia

Davidd drives white-knuckled on the freeway, weaving in and out of slow-moving vehicles, wracked by uncustomary second thoughts. Did he make the right decision? Sure, he saw Ellen on the bus, but was there a passenger next to her? He doesn't know. Did he just leave Rosie, Carlos, and Lita behind to an uncertain fate in Lynnwood to follow his daughter's letter-mate on a wild goose chase?

He tries to tighten his fingers on the wheel, but they're already as stiff as they can get. Second-guessing himself now isn't simply pointless, it's potentially deadly. In The Towers, decisive action, even if it's the wrong action, is always safer than waffling. He pushes all thoughts of Lynnwood out of his mind and focuses on catching up with that bus.

David hunches over the steering wheel, his face close to the glass, but Jimmy, seated next to him, presses himself as far back into the bench seat as he can. He keeps glancing over at David with big, scared eyes, and it's annoying. David should have left

Jimmy on the sidewalk in Lynnwood. But there he goes again, second-guessing himself.

There's a gap in traffic two lanes over that David wants. He glances in his sideview mirror and jerks the wheel to the right, rocketing across both lanes of traffic and cutting off a red sports car.

"Dude!" Jimmy exclaims, unable to take it anymore. "Do you have a death wish? Are you trying to start a police chase?"

David shoots a quick, puzzled look at him, then yanks the wheel to the left to avoid a slow-moving semitruck. "Shut up."

Jimmy throws his hands over his eyes, then drags them down, spreading his fingers and pulling his cheeks into an exaggerated long face. "It's the middle of the day. Cops watch the diamond lane all day long from the overpasses waiting to bust carpool cheaters. Everybody has a damn cell phone, and you're driving like a maniac going a hundred miles an hour in a stolen car. What do you think is going to happen, man?"

David's eyes widen, and he lifts his foot from the gas pedal. The heavy sedan immediately begins decelerating. David knows how to drive, and he's quite good at it, but he's never been on the freeway before. He doesn't know the rules, and that puts him at a severe disadvantage that he hadn't considered. Perhaps it explains why everyone else is going so slow. "What should I do?" he says gruffly.

"The speed limit, for starters," Jimmy says, a tone of snark back in his voice that hasn't been there since David killed his two henchmen.

"Which is?" David asks through gritted teeth.

"Sixty."

David eyes the speedometer, the needle sways near eighty. "Frack." David grunts, but he taps on the brakes. "What else?"

"Get in the diamond lane," Jimmy says confidently.

"That's slower than the others," David protests.

"It won't be in a couple miles. We'll hit the lunch rush and traffic will grind to a halt everywhere but that lane. That lane's just for two-person carpools and buses."

Buses? David jerks the wheel to the left and lumbers into the diamond lane. Behind him, a frustrated driver blares their horn, but David ignores it.

"See that light bar up there?" Jimmy says, pointing to an overpass ahead. "You can barely see it peeking up over the concrete barrier. That's a cop, just like I said."

David swallows hard. If Jimmy hadn't gotten him to slow down, he may have ruined this whole rescue operation.

They glide along in the diamond lane, cruising under the overpass and beyond without incident. "Thanks," David says, the word feeling foreign in his mouth.

Jimmy's prediction is correct. Traffic in all four righthand lanes slows to a crawl as they approach the city limits, but their lane is wide open. "Where are you trying to get to?" Jimmy asks.

"I need to catch up with that bus. Obviously."

"Yeah, well that was a 512, so it's going downtown. I'm not sure if you can follow it. Buses are hard to catch up to. They get all sorts of special rules and routes nobody else can use. If you can't find the bus, where do you want to be?"

"Columbia Tower," David says automatically.

"Easy," Jimmy says. "When we get to the city, if the express lanes are open, take them. If they're not, take the Madison Street exit."

"But I'll miss the bus."

"If the bus uses a special exit, you'll miss it anyway."

Dammit. Everything is one split-second life-or-death decision after another, and David is so tired of it. But Jimmy's right. David knows what the traffic is like downtown. His chances of catching a bus that had a five-minute head start are slim to begin with, and they're non-existent once they hit city streets. "We're going to Columbia."

"Okay, man. The entrance to the parking garage is on the left side of—"

"I know how to get into my own parking garage," David snaps, cutting him off.

"Just trying to help," Jimmy mutters.

And he has helped, as irritating as it is to admit it to himself. David drives the rest of the way to Columbia Tower in silence. He never planned to let Jimmy go alive. He's a zed, he's dead anyway, and David doesn't like the idea of a loose end out there, especially not one with a vendetta, but perhaps now he owes Jimmy something?

David circles around multiple levels of the parking garage before finally finding a spot just barely wide enough to accommodate the Buick. He throws the car in park and gestures at Jimmy. "Get out."

"Okay, man, well, thanks for the ride. I'll be going now?" Jimmy's obviously trying to sound self-assured, but his voice lifts at the end, turning his statement into a question.

David pulls his knife out of his pocket and Jimmy visibly quakes. But instead of gutting him with it, David walks to the back end of the car and jams it into the lock on the back of the trunk. He twists, and the trunk swings open.

David indicates the open trunk with two flicks of his wrist. "Inside."

"Aw, man," Jimmy whines. "Can't you just let me go? I did what you wanted. I found Lita."

No, he hadn't, he found Ellen, but David isn't interested in arguing with him. Jimmy gets to survive this encounter because of his assistance on the freeway and no other reason. David doesn't need to tell him that, though. "I might need you later," he says. And it's true. He might. He probably won't, but he might.

"What if you don't?"

"Like you said, it's a stolen car. Someone will find you eventually."

"Damn, man, it's gonna be hot and stuffy."

Jimmy has no idea what hot and stuffy feels like when you're working under protective sheeting on the roof on a Burn Level Five day. "I can kill you after you get in the trunk if you prefer," David says dryly.

Gulping, Jimmy dives into the trunk.

"If we don't see each other again, Squint, don't ever try to find me."

"Are you kidding me? If I see you again, I'm turning around and running the other way." Jimmy pants.

David purses his lips. Jimmy Squint will run again someday. The futuristic healing compound David shoved in his wound will see to that. But additional medical care to prevent infection wouldn't hurt.

Jimmy curls into a ball and hugs his knees to his chest. Another car crests the parking level and chugs slowly past. Certainly, Jimmy must hear it too. But he doesn't move a muscle, just stays huddled with his eyes squeezed shut tightly.

David reaches into the trunk as if he's tucking away valuables and nods at the other driver. The driver nods back, oblivious to the fact that David holds the life of another human being in his hands. David wrinkles his brow. He's not used to feeling merciful, and it's an odd sensation. He cocks his head, remembering the last riot he quelled in The Towers. He was merciful then too, wasn't he? Odd.

"The Harborview Emergency entrance is at Ninth and James," David says gruffly. Spinning on his heel, he walks away, leaving the trunk wide open.

Goodbye, Jimmy Squint. For your sake, may we never meet again.

CHAPTER TWENTY-SEVEN

July 8, 2018 – Rosie

I'm not sure if I'll ever get used to elevators, but the sense of dread I normally experience when I'm in an elevator shaft is nowhere to be found. I'm so excited to see my dad that the ride up to the fortieth floor feels interminable, but for different reasons than normal.

As soon as I step off the elevator, though, I remember what happened the last time I was here. It was only a few days ago that I wrote, "Help me Daddy" on the mural I'm walking slowly past. And there it is, the thick black marker popping out at me from the lower right corner of the picture. I feel like a totally different person from that desperate girl who scrawled out those words, not even knowing why she was writing them.

I'm still a desperate girl, but now it's for legitimate and known reasons. But soon, all that worry and stress will fall away. I'm going home.

I hear the voice of the barista from around the corner, calling out a name, and I wince. It sounds just like the guy who was working here the day I defaced the mural. What if he recognizes me?

"Ellen," I hiss, and she stops just before the wide entrance to the coffee shop.

"What?" she asks.

"I have a bit of a…history with this place. If I have to run, you and Dad and should meet me on the top floor of Smith Tower."

She nods. "Roger that."

My heart does a little flip flop at her words. Barely anybody uses that expression here, but in just a little while, I'll be back where we all do. Where commands are issued in barking tones because we have no time to waste and hesitation often results in death.

I nod, and together, we round the corner.

My eyes drink in the people seated at the tables, sipping their coffees, tapping on phones and laptops. One person reads a newspaper, like it's 1996 or something. But none of these people are my father.

"Ellen?" I ask questioningly.

"Maybe he's in the bathroom."

"I think I might have ruined the public restroom privileges for everyone," I mutter.

"He's here," she insists. "Sit over there and wait. I'll get us a couple of coffees."

All the dread that I didn't experience in the elevator was apparently poised in a wave over my head because it just crashed over top of me and now it's trying to drown me.

I walk woodenly to a corner table next to the window and sink into a chair. If that coffee guy does recognize me and security chases me again, will I even be able to run? My limbs feel like waterlogged timbers. Where is my father? Ellen still insists on saying he's here, even though he's clearly not.

I watch Ellen in line, but my eyes also continuously scan the entrance. If Dad's in the bathroom like Ellen suggested, he'll come through that door any second. I glance around at all the other tables. No single coffee cups sit unattended. My father is not here. Something went wrong. That, or Ellen lied.

No! Why on Earth would Ellen lie to me? The idea is preposterous and I feel disloyal even thinking it.

There's a long line of zeds in front of Ellen, waiting their turns to ask something of the man in the green apron. At least he's so busy, he's not likely to notice me, and if he does, he might not connect me with the homeless teenager who took his pen and damaged the mural. I'm a lot taller now, and my whole shape has changed. I'm curvier, and my hair is longer and healthier. It's legitimately possible that he won't recognize me.

"Ah, a tall drip coffee for my most loyal customer," the barista cries out. He hands a cup to the man at the front of the line, who turns and surveys the room with a look of hopeless despair on his weathered face, and my heart stops.

"Daddy?" I whisper, then louder. "Daddy? Dad!"

I stood up without realizing it, and now the entire café is looking at me. So much for flying under the radar, but I don't care.

"Rosie!" my father shouts. He shoves his cup of coffee into the unsuspecting hands of the person behind him in line and charges through the throng of people lining up to order their own beverages. I stand trembling but otherwise incapable of movement. My dad covers all the distance between us in a matter of seconds and throws his arms around me. "Rosie!"

I hug him back and sob, tears streaming down my face the way they never could in our own time. And what's even weirder is Dad is crying too, rivers of moisture etching the dry creek beds of his face. I've never seen him cry.

He kisses the top of my head over and over and crushes me to his chest. I nestle in and breathe in the familiar scent of my dad, a mixture of salt, sea, and earth that always makes me think of safety and love. People around us go, "Aww," and lower their voices to whispers, like they're in a library. When Dad finally lets me go, all the people around us are smiling. If anybody from security tried to show up and throw me out now, I think there'd be an uprising. Dad sniffs and swallows. He keeps his hands on my shoulders and takes a half-step back from me, his eyes scanning me up and down. "My god, Rosie. You're here. You're alive. Are you hurt?"

I shake my head. Not on the outside, which is what I'm sure he means.

Ellen glides by and sets two steaming paper cups of coffee on our table, then discreetly takes a table of her own across the room. She chooses a station close to the entrance, but one that still gives her an unobstructed view of the entire café, like a good sentry should.

Dad and I sit down at our corner table, his back against the north wall, mine against the west. He holds my left hand in his right, as if he's afraid that if he lets me go, I might bob away like flotsam. He picks up his coffee and takes a slow sip. I do the same.

"I got here late today," Dad says. "I've been here every day, waiting for Ellen to bring you to me, but today I was late. I thought I'd missed you."

"Ellen told me you were here. When you weren't, I doubted her for a second," I say, and my eyes brim with tears again. I doubted my letter-mate. What kind of a person have I become? Will The Towers even want me anymore? Am I a fitting citizen, after all this time in the past?

Dad must read my thoughts. "Survival is different here. Things that are unquestionable in The Towers, well…we don't have a guarantee that those translate after travel." He glances at Ellen, where she pointedly looks away from us, her eyes scanning the room, searching for threats. Dad refocuses on me. "Ellen earned your trust in our time, and she earned my trust here. I've offered her a position in our family and she accepted."

I gasp, and my right hand flies to cover my mouth. "Really? She didn't tell me." I can feel my whole face begin to glow with a light shining out from inside me.

"Yes," Dad confirms. "She is my niece and your cousin. She will live full-time in our quarters once we return."

I nod. "I want that," I say. But the mention of our quarters and who will be living there hits me like a sneaker wave. "What about Sarah? What happened to her?"

"Who?" Dad says, and I feel my eyes pop open in astonishment.

"Sarah," I say slowly, overenunciating the name. "Your wife? My stepmother? She's the whole reason why I'm here in the first place."

"Oh my god, Rosie," Dad says, his breathing becoming rapid and shallow. He shakes his head, like he's trying to clear it. "Sometimes I forget all about her, like she's not real. I don't even remember why I married her."

"Oh, she's very real," I say. "And she proved it by pushing me down an elevator shaft."

"I know. I have her zip-tied in our quarters. At this point, I'm not even sure how long she's been there. She may be dead. I kept her alive in case she could provide any more details about your disappearance."

I pull my hand out of Dad's and lace my fingers together tightly on the table in front of us. "I can give you all the details you need. She waited for me on the twenty-fifth floor and when my mission got aborted she stopped me in the stairwell and said you needed me to meet you on the roof. I thought it was something to do with the Achtung and I leaned out into the shaft, thinking I was going to be winched up, and she pushed me in."

Dad winces, but I go on.

"I climbed up the shaft, back to twenty-five, but she was still there. She kicked me in the face before I could pull myself onto the floor and I went down again."

"Oh, Rosie." Dad covers my interlocked fingers with both of his hands.

"I knew I couldn't climb all the way to the roof, so my only other option was down and out. I swam to the bottom and made it all the way out of the building. I was going to swim to the surface, climb in through a window, and find you. But I got caught on debris underwater near the seafloor." I close my eyes, remembering my panic and the feeling of certain death, how my lungs screamed to take a breath, please just take a breath, even if it was nothing but foul seawater, it would be satisfying if just for a brief, heart-stopping moment. I shudder and open my eyes and focus on my father's anguished face. "I almost drowned, Daddy. You know I'm not that great at packing my lungs, but I was down there for a long time. A personal best, I'm sure. But I was stuck and about to die. I knew I was almost out of time. And that was when I remembered."

Dad squeezes my hands and nods along with my story, like he knows it already, but he wants to hear it from me.

"Lisa and Doug prepped me for my mission, and when it was aborted I gave Doug back my outbound travel chemicals, but not the ones for my return." I speed up, my voice rushed. "And I know that was a severe breach of protocol by all of us, but, Daddy, if Lisa or Doug had taken them or if I'd remembered to give them back, I'd be dead right now."

Dad stares at me, unblinking, his voice like ground gravel. "You're right. It was an extreme oversight. And thank god for it. No one will be receiving disciplinary action in this matter. Lisa and Doug deserve a goddamn medal for foresight if you want to know my opinion."

I take a deep breath and slowly blow it out. Lisa or Doug could have been thrown off the roof for what happened, despite the ultimately life-saving outcome, and I'm so glad my dad sees it the same way I do.

"Ellen will be moving into our quarters and Sarah will be

moving out. I've found you now. I no longer need to keep her alive for any reason. I'll throw her off the roof myself when we return. Unless you'd like to?" Dad raises his eyebrows at me.

It's the first time he's mentioned us going home, and my eyes must fill with tears again because Dad's face wavers in front of me. It's surprising. After all the crying I've done today, I figured my tear ducts would have run dry by now. I nod. I would like to be the one to push her off the roof. An unbidden image of Carlos pops into my mind. He always tried to convince me that I was such a good person. Boy, did he have me pegged wrong.

I tell Carlos's memory to get lost and shove his gentle, smiling face out of my thoughts. "How did you know where I was?" I ask my dad. "I mean, when? And why did you send Ellen to find me? Did you get my note?"

"The box where I receive all my Achtungs is gone. I don't know when it disappeared. If you left a message in there, it must have vanished sometime recently. What day did you leave the message?"

"July 2nd."

Dad sighs. "That date and everything since has been thoroughly trampled by chrononauts. We may never know what happened."

"General Safeco was there," I blurt out.

Dad's eyebrows zoom to the top of his head. "Safeco?"

"Yes!" I exclaim. "Remember, you told me he was a chrononaut? Well, this is where he was lost for all those years. My friend Carlos knew him as a homeless man named Old Dirty Plastered, or ODP for short. But it was General Safeco, and when he stepped out onto the top floor of Smith Tower right after I put a note for you in the box, I was so shocked. I was like, 'General Safeco?' and in a second he shifted from this confused and pissed-off homeless guy to the general. The next thing I knew, he whipped out a syringe and plunged. He must have had it on him all those years. He dematerialized right in front of me. When we get back, I have to talk to him."

I'm feeling pretty emotional, and my eyes must water again, because Dad seems to waver in front of me. I look over at Ellen, and I can see right through her. She's there, but it's like she's made out of vapor. I squeeze my eyes shut hard and pop them open. She's back to normal. I must have imagined that.

Dad's face darkens. "We need to have a long talk about Safeco when we get back. But right now I want to hear about this Carlos. Your friend? Isn't he the man who kidnapped you?"

Now I feel like my eyes are going to pop out of my head. "Carlos? Kidnap me? No, Dad, he saved my life. Like, multiple times. He took me to the hospital when I would have died on the street from an infection in my port. He broke me out of the hospital when they were going to arrest me on drug charges. I didn't know who I was, Dad – my memory was gone for weeks – I traveled here half-drowned with no helmet. My brain was a stewed tomato. He kept me safe. He cares…*cared* about me."

Dad's eyes have been growing bigger and rounder this whole time. "Ellen told me he took you."

"Then she was wrong. Or misinformed."

We both glance over at Ellen, but she still looks studiously away.

"Ellen seemed so sure and she's not one to make mistakes."

"I guess there was this time that Carlos gave somebody the slip on the bus – he thought we were being followed by this girl named Lita – but she turned out to be Ellen. That would explain why Ellen thought he took me. He's actually…" I blink back fresh tears. God, will I ever be normal again? "Really nice."

Dad's face has gone from red to white to red again during the short time I've been talking, and it looks like he wants to say about nine different things, but maybe it's the break in my voice that stops him, I don't know.

"I'm glad you don't feel like you were kidnapped," he says tightly.

"I wasn't kidnapped," I stress. "Carlos was a very special person to me."

Dad nods curtly. "That's another thing we can talk about when we get home, if you'd like."

I'm not sure if I'm ever going to feel like talking about that, but I nod glumly and stare at the table. I look up at Dad through my lashes and he has that wavery look again before he snaps into focus.

I swear there are no tears in my eyes. I look over at Ellen. She's transparent again. She wavers, then seems to solidify.

A horrible feeling takes hold in the pit of my stomach, and I have to try something. "After we get back," I start, keeping my eyes fixed on Ellen. The instant the words are out of my mouth, she shimmers, goes transparent, and for a millisecond, I swear she's not there at all. Then she snaps back into focus.

"What?" Dad says, startling me.

"What?" I answer stupidly.

"After we get back, what?" Dad prods.

"I don't remember," I say absently.

Dad nods, then glances around the café. "We've been here too long, Rosie. It's time to go home. Knowing that Safeco was here in unnerving. So was your mention of this 'Lita' person. And you think Lita is actually Ellen? That's a thread I need to pull on when we return. But every minute we stay here is another minute that disaster could strike. My mother – your grandmother – is somewhere nearby. Can you imagine what a catastrophe that would be if we crossed paths with her?"

I nod, and I watch as Dad blinks in and out a couple times in front of my eyes, like a lamp with a loosely connected bulb. Every time I think about going home, he disappears. His fear of crossing paths with his mother is valid because it's true. I am his mother. And if I go home, he will never exist. And neither will Ellen.

Dad stands up and helps me to my feet. He puts his arms around me one more time and hugs me close. "God, Rosie, I'm so sorry about everything. I spent so much time looking for you in 2007 when you were here the whole time. I never got your note in Smith Tower. To make matters worse, I didn't complete my written mission notes before we were interrupted by the Achtung. I forgot about the box I asked you to install in the Seattle Municipal Tower so I never received any communications you put there. I hate myself for that."

Holy shit. My heart races and my mind zooms back to Dad's mission briefing just before I ran downstairs to the prep room and this whole thing started. And I remember vividly. He told me to get tetanus boosters, sanitary napkins, and to paint a wall blue. But before all that, he'd told me to install a communications box in Muni. It was supposed to be my choice on the location as long as it was the twentieth floor or higher. I was going to tell him where I'd chosen to install the box when I returned. It was supposed to be a backup communications box, I'm sure of it. But it wasn't on my written objective list. Dad just relayed it to me verbally, then we went off on a tangent about Safeco being a traveler, and I forgot all about it until this moment. My god.

"Where did you end up installing that box, Rosie?" Dad asks.

I didn't. I didn't install it at all. I stare at him, trying to memorize every line in his face, every pore in his skin, the special softness in his eyes that's only for me, the daughter he loves, and I come to my final decision. "Thirty-ninth floor. West facing wall," I say faintly.

"Good. I'll recover it when we get home. We can read your letters together, and you can fill in details and tell me everything that happened."

I nod, but I say nothing because my throat is choked with tears and pain and terror and a loss so profound, I can't speak.

Dad and Ellen are going home; they belong there. But I am not. I am Rosarita Columbia, my father's daughter, but also his mother. If I leave this world, no one will step in to take on my responsibilities. Dad and Ellen wavering in and out of existence is all the proof I need of that. My future is already written. My life is here, in the past.

"Let's go home, Rosie."

This time, when I nod and agree, I'm lying. I won't plunge my chemicals and follow them home. And fate knows I mean it because Dad stays as solid and real as he's ever been. Ellen joins us and she's real too. I reach out and take Dad's hand as we walk across the café, like I'm a little girl again. I'll only be his daughter for a few more minutes, and I want to soak up every drop of his love that I can during that time. Because I'll never see my father again. The next time I see David Columbia, he'll be my son.

CHAPTER TWENTY-EIGHT

July 8, 2018 – Ellen

Rosie and David talk intently and I watch them out of the corner of my eye sometimes, but mostly I try to give them their privacy. They're not going to get past me, seated in the corner the way they are, so my job is to protect them. I'm the lookout and the guard, and I take my job seriously.

A couple of times when I do glance over their way, I catch fleeting looks from Rosie, and I wonder if they're talking about me because the look on her face is really strange.

I have so many things to answer for, and I will. I'll tell them everything. I'll come completely clean and I'll place the blame squarely where it belongs. On General Safeco. And, I have to admit, on myself. I never should have just trusted him and gone off on a mission – a time travel mission, no less – without clearance from the president.

When Rosie and David rise from their table, I stand too, and when I join them and move toward the stairwell, Rosie tries to smile at me, but she looks so, so sad that I know when we get back to 2074 I'm totally in for it.

Uncle David – can I even call him that anymore? – smiles at me, though. It's a broad grin showing all his teeth, and I'm taken aback. Why does Rosie look nauseated, but David grins at me like I just completed my final climb? "Thank you, Ellen," Uncle David says warmly. "Thank you for finding my girl."

Rosie misses a step on the staircase and stumbles. What is going on with her? David steadies her and I look at their linked hands. Rosie is gripping her father's hand so tightly, her knuckles are white.

"We plunge from the twenty-first floor stairwell," David says in a low voice. It's the safest floor for arrival in our time. From there we'll go straight to the prep room to debrief and plan out next steps."

"Sounds good," I say, because I'm not sure what else to say. Next steps? Going by the look on Rosie's face, the next step is a funeral. But judging by the expression on Uncle David's face, we all have something exciting to look forward to.

I can't reconcile the difference between the two of them, their moods and their mannerisms, but I don't think Uncle David notices. Now that he's in 'get it done' mode, he's unstoppable.

Together, we hurry down multiple flights of stairs. Rosie doesn't miss any more steps; her gait is much more assured now. When we reach the landing, Rosie lets go of her father's hand and comes over to me. She touches my face gently with both hands, one on either side, and she looks at me for a long moment, then she tips her forehead to mine. "I love you, Ellen," she whispers.

What is going on here? "I...I love you too," I say.

Uncle David passes out three syringes, his eyes darting all over the stairwell in every direction, making sure we don't get interrupted, I guess.

"We have to do this quick – before someone comes," David says, confirming my suspicions.

He pulls out three syringes and looks at them critically. He passes the first one to Rosie. "I calibrated this one for you. You're taller and heavier than I expected, but it'll get you to early April at least. Just hunker down in your room and wait for me to come get you if you arrive days ahead of me." She wraps her fingers around the syringe carefully.

"This is yours," Uncle David says, handing a hypodermic needle to me. "Do you have a port?"

When I traveled here, General Safeco administered a shot in my carotid artery. "I don't know what that means," I say.

"You don't then," David replies.

"My port is gone too," Rosie says.

"What?" David exclaims.

"It was removed when I was hospitalized. It was infected," Rosie explains. "I can administer the shot myself in the carotid artery, just like Ellen will." We all know how to give ourselves lifesaving shots; it's part of basic training. This is one lifesaving shot I'm sure our instructors never thought of, but it goes in the exact same way.

David chews his lip. "Do you want me to do it for you?"

"No!" Rosie cries, way too forcefully. "I hear someone coming," she says hurriedly. "We need to go."

David nods. "Okay. Spread out."

Rosie takes up a post in the northern quadrant of the stair-well. I take south, and David is between us in the western position.

"You don't have ports, so it isn't the typical process, only a plunge. I'll count us down," David says. He tightens his grip on his hypodermic and Rosie and I do too.

Rosie raises the hypodermic to her neck. Her hand trembles, but it's so slight that I wonder if Uncle David notices.

Something is wrong with her. I let my eyes drift until they're almost closed, like I'm deep in my own head, but I'm really watching her. Rosie doesn't realize the scrutiny she's under. And something is definitely off.

The vein throbs in her neck, her heart is pounding, but her

chest barely moves. I don't know how she's pumping that much blood through her body without breathing, but she's doing it. She needs to watch out or she's going to faint.

David zips a pocket open in his vest to reveal his own skin. He quickly peels back a piece of flesh-colored tape, and now I know what he meant by a port. A device is imbedded underneath his skin with an opening for his needle. He inserts the tip into the device. "Ready?"

Rosie and I both nod.

David takes a deep breath. "On three."

He shoves the hypodermic fully into the port. Rosie and I insert our needles into our own necks.

"Two."

He touches his thumb to the plunging end. Rosie and I do too.

"One." He jams his thumb down.

Rosie lifts her thumb from the plunger end and jerks the hypodermic out of her neck. I'm so shocked, I almost plunge my needle reflexively, but at the last second I stop myself. Rosie isn't watching me, though; she's throwing herself across the stairwell landing, closing the distance between herself and her father.

"I'm sorry, Daddy. I love you. I love you so much!" She throws her arms around him and tries to hug him, but he's mostly vapor. His eyes are round and his mouth is open in a soundless O as his body disintegrates.

Rosie doesn't even look my way; she just clutches her hypodermic and sprints down the stairs, screaming "I love you" and running as if she's being chased by a thousand demons.

But she's only being chased by one.

Me.

CHAPTER TWENTY-NINE

July 8, 2018 – Ellen

Nobody can beat Rosie on stairs in The Towers, and that holds true in 2018 as well. But in a footrace on flat ground, I've got the advantage. My legs are longer and I've always had better breath control. Rosie's fast, but I'm faster.

Still, this isn't the treadmill in a training session. These are city streets with dawdling pedestrians, racing cars, and ill-timed lights that seem determined to cause my untimely death.

Rosie's prowess on the stairs gave her a two-block lead, but I haven't lost sight of her. She darts and weaves through the throngs of zeds that surge toward Westlake Center. If she makes it there before me, she has a legitimate chance of shaking me off.

"Rosie!" I yell for the hundredth time, wasting precious breath, letting her gain another half-step advantage. She doesn't look back, just plows forward, knocking zeds out of her way, spinning them around in her wake. They shout, "Hey!" and "Watch it!" and stuff like that, possibly drowning out my voice. But Rosie doesn't flinch.

She's the one who just ran out on her dad when we were all

supposed to travel back to our home in 2074, back to safety. *And also back to soul-crushing loneliness, boredom, and pain*, my brain whispers. I block that voice out. I have no time for the burden of those types of thoughts.

The light ahead of me turns red and cars zip through the intersection, gunning their engines to crest the series of steep hills leading up from the waterfront.

I pick up speed too, my legs pounding the pavement as fast as they can go. I can't stop and wait for this light to change; I'll lose her for sure. I charge into the intersection against the light. Tires squeal. One driver either doesn't see me or doesn't care that I'm there. I leap and land my butt on the hood of the car, sliding and using my momentum to carry me the rest of the way across the street. I hit the ground running. I've made up distance on Rosie.

"Rosie!" I yell again, and this time she looks back over her shoulder, but she doesn't break stride. If anything, she puts her head down and runs harder, opening up a little more distance between us. She's nearly to the decorative brick that paves the Westlake Center shopping area. If she gets there, she can melt into the crowd in a thousand different directions. Maybe just yelling 'Rosie' isn't enough.

"Rosarita Columbia!" I scream.

Rosie's legs both seem to freeze for a moment, as if her knees have locked up, and she stumbles. Staggering, she crashes into a medium-sized man clad in tan chinos and a polo shirt. They both go down hard. That's all the time I need to fly to her side.

The man and Rosie are all tangled up. "Get off me, you piece of trash," he cries, wiggling and shoving from underneath her. He curls his fingers around his phone and uses that hand to chop her in the neck. She cries out and tries to rise to her feet, but her legs are snarled in the strap of his messenger bag.

Roaring, I twist the guy's green polo shirt in my left fist and raise his torso off the sidewalk. I punch him three times in the face in quick succession. On the last blow, one of his front teeth breaks and I cut my knuckle on it. I wipe my bloody fist on the leg of my pants, grab Rosie under the arms, and haul her up. She struggles against me, wild-eyed, but I lock my hands around her upper arms and give her a shake. That seems to loosen her tongue more than anything because she screeches as she fights. "I can't go back, Ellen. You can't make me. You have to let me go."

"You can't stay here for Carlos. It's over, Rosie," I say in a firm, authoritative voice.

"It's not that!" Rosie cries, and her eyes roll around in terror.

Scaring her is the exact opposite of what I'm trying to do. I keep my hands tight on her, but I alter my tone of voice. "There's no future for us here, Rosie," I say softly.

"There's no future for anyone if I leave this time," she yells. "Don't you get it? Didn't you feel it back in The Tower when I was talking to my dad? Every time I made a firm decision to go back, you'd vanish, Ellen. Gone!"

She's not struggling in my grip anymore, so I take a chance and loosen the vise-like clamp of my fingers. "I had a few moments of disorientation back in the Columbia Tower café," I admit. "But I was just hungry."

"You weren't hungry, or thirsty, or over-caffeinated, Ellen, you ceased to exist. Just for a moment. But as soon as I flip-flopped and second-guessed myself about going back, you'd pop back into reality."

"This is nuts." On the ground beside us, the man I punched unconscious emits a loud groan, and I realize people are standing all around us staring. "What, have you never seen a guy get his ass kicked by a girl before? Move along, losers," I bark at them, and most of them heed my command, but a couple of guys don't, and one pulls out a phone. "We have to get out of here, Rosie," I say out of the corner of my mouth.

"That's what I'm trying to do," she wails plaintively, not helping our case at all. "The Towers will never happen if Dad finds me and sends me back. But where can I go? Every place I can think of, he'll think of too."

I don't know if she's snapped and gone insane or what, but I chose my path when I failed to plunge my chemicals. For better or worse, I'm with Rosie. "I know a place. I'll take you there."

Fifteen minutes later, Rosie and I sit cross-legged at the top of the Volunteer Park water tower. I found this spot months ago. It's a public space, but it's always deserted, and I knew Rosie would feel safe here. The irregular brick exterior is great when you need to satisfy the urge to climb. I didn't want to attract attention, though, so we didn't scale the outside. We climbed the hundred-plus stairs to get up here like a regular couple of zeds.

The whole way here, I was half-sure Rosie was going to take off – I could read in her body language that she was thinking about it – but she never bolted. She trusted me all the way up here, so now it's time for me to trust her.

"Tell me why you didn't go back," I say. "Tell me everything."

So she does. She pours out the entire story, starting with her stepmother pushing her down the straws, to landing on Carlos's tent, to escaping the hospital and regaining her memories, and finally to realizing she isn't just named after her grandmother – she is her grandmother.

Rosie is her grandmother? The famous Rosarita Columbia is my letter-mate? It takes a while for that to sink in.

Word by word, she shreds all my doubts into smithereens and I see the terrible truth of it all. I gasp when the reality of her being Rosarita Columbia – that Rosarita Columbia – hits me. "You're David's daughter…and his mother?"

She nods miserably. "I love him so much. It kills me to do this to him. But if I don't, he dies. And so do you, and so does every other citizen who has lived in The Towers for the last fifty-six years. You would never even be born, Ellen. I can't go home, because I have to build everything that we call home. This is my life now. Forever."

I rise to my feet and pull her to hers, and together we stare out the west-facing windows of the water tower, watching the sun go down. Neither of us speaks for a long time, then she finally breaks the silence. "I was really scared to tell you all that," Rosie whispers. "Carlos knows, and I figured it was okay because he…well, because he's from now." Her voice grows stronger. "The future doesn't affect him the same way. But since you're from then, I was terrified to say anything. And to be honest, I thought you might be tricking me and that you were going to jab me with your set of return chemicals and send me back by force."

"I would never do that to you."

"My father told me he offered you a family tie. That you're my cousin now."

Moths flutter in my stomach. "Yes," I say, swallowing hard as the enormity of everything I lost by staying here with Rosie mushrooms in my mind. "I am your cousin. Your dad isn't here, but we are truly family now and nothing changes that."

"I thought that your loyalty might lie more with him than me."

I raise myself to my full height, straightening my spine verte-brae by vertebrae, then dip to one knee and clutch her hand, looking up at her. "I'm loyal to you, Rosarita Columbia. I always have been, and I always will be."

She squeezes my hand and with gentle pressure pulls me to my feet. "I love you, Ellen."

"I love you too, Rosie."

We fall silent for another long stretch of time. My mind is a whirlpool of thoughts, one idea after another swirling around in my head, only to be sucked away into an empty unknown vortex.

"I thought I'd have to do this alone," Rosie says in a small voice as the last light of day fades away. "And I wasn't sure what to do. I still don't know what direction to go in, but I'm so glad I'm not the only one who can hold the compass."

"I will never leave your side," I vow.

Rosie takes a deep breath, bites her lip, and obviously struggles with whether to say the words that come out of her mouth next. "You can go back, Ellen," she says haltingly. "And you probably should."

"What?"

Rosie looks like she wants to throw up, but she forces out the explanation. "If you were by my side during The Collapse, there would be legends about you. We would all know your name. We would sing your praises and thank every god that no one believes in anymore for your strength and resilience. But we don't. After I told you everything, I expected new memories. I expected to remember stories I'd learned growing up, about Rosarita and Ellen, the two women who prepared for the unimaginable and saved humanity. But it's still only me."

I quirk my mouth up a smidge. "Maybe I'm just more humble than you are."

Rosie bursts out laughing, and then she spins and throws her arms around me in a huge hug. "Thank you."

I hug her back and chuckle. My laugh sounds odd and rusty to me, but it feels good. "I'm serious, though. Maybe I'm just more of a silent partner," I say after our mirth has petered out.

"I don't think so," she says, shaking her head. "But will you stay and help me for a while?"

"Rosie, I told you, I'm not leaving. Of course I'll help you."

She tilts her head, and I can tell she wants to argue with me some more but decides against it. "You still have your chemicals, though, right?" she says.

"Yeah." I pat the pocket of my vest, and my heartrate triples when I realize what else is in there.

She pulls her own hypodermic out of her pocket and it rests on her open palm. "I don't." She shakes her hand and the syringe drops to the ground. She lifts her foot and stomps on it, smashing the plastic tubing and grinding it under her foot.

"Rosie!" I gasp.

"I can't keep it. It's too dangerous. And maybe too tempting. I can never go back."

Tears tremble on her lashes and I pull her close, holding her and stroking her hair while she cries.

And I'm sad for her, but as soon as my hand went to my vest pocket and I felt the dual lumps in there, the urge to cry left me completely. Because I don't only have the return chemicals Uncle David gave me. No one knows, but I have a syringe from General Safeco too. Maybe Rosie's right and I do return home. A smile curls across my lips. Maybe Jordan and I have a future after all.

Rosie can't run from The Collapse; it's her destiny. But is Rosarita Columbia – the woman who saved humanity – a myth? How can Rosie prepare for the disaster that's months away with only one friend by her side? Turn the page for a sneak peek at FADE TO BLACK

PENELOPE WRIGHT

FADE TO

THE COLLAPSE — BOOK FIVE

BLACK

SNEAK PEEK AT FADE TO BLACK

Part One

July 8, 2018 – Ellen

Neither Rosie nor I are prepared for the outdoors. We have no tent, no sleeping bags or blankets, not even a pile of newspaper. I thought we'd spend the night here, on the observation deck floor of the water tower in Volunteer Park, but when the sun is fully below the horizon, other people show up with syringes of their own, and they're definitely not here to time travel.

"I can make 'em leave," I growl, but Rosie puts her hand on my arm.

"Please don't cause a scene. I have to fly under the radar. We can't attract any attention."

I grumble and glare at the even-more-zombie-like-than-normal zeds who loll about, poking themselves with hypodermic needles, but I do as she says. I have no delusions that I'm in charge here. Rosie's in command and I'm her lieutenant. If she says we go, we go.

We exit the water tower, cross the lawn, and find a small

hollow in a cluster of bushes, just big enough for both of us, but do we really want to stay here all night?

"Let's stretch out on the lawn before we squeeze in there for the night," Rosie says.

"We can make our way to the bunker," I suggest. There's a secret waystation underneath Aurora Avenue, in an old, closed-off pedestrian underpass. I've used it before, and so has Rosie, but she shakes her head so vehemently, her hair flies in clouds around her face. She clutches her chest like she's having a coronary.

"No. What you have to understand," she says when she's finally stopped spluttering, "is that we can't go anywhere my dad might look for me."

"So we can't go anywhere then? Your dad loves you, and he's driven. He's going to look everywhere. He'll never stop."

"I've been thinking about that. For right now, we need to avoid any of the places he'll check for me first. But pretty soon, he'll have to stop looking for me in 2018. He won't have any choice."

"What do you mean? Nobody tells your dad what to do."

"You're right. Nobody's going to intercede and try to stop him. No person, that is. But the thing about time travel is there are laws that we've discovered. And one of them is that you can't be in the same place as yourself at the same time."

"Yeah, but I know that your dad never looked for you in 2018 before. He told me that. He's not going to run into himself here."

"He will. Another version of him is going to show up soon, and that version, I think, will supersede any time traveling version of himself."

Rosie's not making any sense and I wonder if she's being purposely vague. I flash back to General Safeco and his warnings before he sent me here. *We don't speak of time travel.* Well, Rosie and I are certainly smashing that rule to smithereens now, aren't we? "I don't get it," I say. "But I need to understand this stuff completely if I'm going to help and support you. I know we're not supposed to talk about time travel, but we're both here, in the past, and we both know exactly what's up. I don't think it's going to ruin the future for you to be straight with me from here on out."

Rosie bites her lip and her eyes dart around. Her inability to make snap judgements was always embarrassing for her, back in The Towers, where decisiveness is highly valued. In our world, the wrong decision, made quickly, is better than taking too long to think things over and dying. But she's getting better at it, because after a few seconds, her eyes focus on mine and she speaks clearly. "My dad was two days old on the day of The Collapse. Which means that very soon, he'll be a fetus in some woman's uterus. And the first law of time travel will kick into effect. He won't be allowed to be in two places at once."

I shake my head. "It must not work the way you think. A litter cycle takes a whole year. If you were right about that law thing, your dad would have been incubating for three months already and couldn't possibly have been here earlier today."

Rosie plucks a few blades of grass and sifts them through her fingers. "They don't have litter cycles yet. Most women are still fertile. They don't grow the next generation once a year in plas-tissue sacs. In 2018 it only takes about forty weeks to grow a zygote to completion. Some take a little longer, some a little less. But if my dad is an unremarkable fetus, he'll be conceived somewhere around July twenty-second."

"Your father's the President of the United Towers. I'm not sure anyone would ever accuse him of having been an unremark-able fetus," I say doubtfully.

Rosie lifts a shoulder. "If he was born early, he would have been too fragile to survive The Collapse. I suppose he could have been born late, but all that means for me is that he'll be conceived even earlier, which is a good thing. But I'm not counting on that. In these days any time a woman went more than about a week after her due date, they'd give her drugs to make her go into labor."

"Labor?"

"It's where your body contracts and the woman literally pushes the baby out the exit, using her internal muscles."

I shudder at the gross thought. "That's so weird. They're way safer inside than out. You'd think they'd try to keep them in."

"Not in 2018. A year-old fetus would be way too big. The mother would die."

I shake my head. "So if you're right—"

"I'm right," Rosie insists.

"Like I said, if you're right, we only need to lie low for a couple of weeks, and after that we can go to the bunker."

"It's not as simple as that. My dad might send somebody else to find me. Like the opposite of an assassin, but if they find me and 'save' me"—she mimes little air quotes—"then everyone dies."

I stopped breathing the moment Rosie used the word 'assassin,' but she doesn't notice because she's too fixated on what she's saying now. "He'd have them check the bunker, Smith Tower, and Columbia Towers for sure. Probably the library, plus a couple other places I can think of. I'd be the prime target, but they'll be looking for you too. We both need to fly under the radar."

I nod. Rosie doesn't know I was sent here by General Safeco to assassinate her. She's in more danger than she realizes. Yes, her father might send the 'opposite of an assassin,' as she called it, but Safeco might send a real one. He already has, and he must know by now that I abandoned my original mission.

I know why Rosie can't go back home to our time. She's not just an ordinary teenage girl. She's Rosarita Columbia, the founder of our world and the savior of humanity. She may be from 2074, but she'll live the rest of her life here in the past, preparing The Towers to support life when The Collapse happens. On April 19, 2019, a secret nuclear base will explode and Antarctica will flash melt instantly.

The sea level will rise hundreds of feet overnight. Coastal nuclear reactors all over the world will melt down. I understand why her father would send a rescue squad for Rosie. He thinks he's saving her from The Collapse. What I don't understand is why Safeco wants her dead. Is he trying to destroy our world? Rosie is the one who had the foresight to predict The Collapse and prepare for it.

My heart skips a beat. Can it be called foresight? Or is it hindsight? She and I were both born in 2056. We grew up in the United Towers, in the aftermath of The Collapse, where Rosie's dad, David Columbia, is president. David is Rosarita's son, raised by his mother to lead our society.

I feel dizzy and I thrust my hands into the dewy grass on either side of me to regain my balance. Rosie looks at me sympathetically.

"It's crazy, huh?"

I wet my lips with my tongue and nod.

"Dad was always worried about causing a conundrum," Rosie says morosely. "Turns out, my whole life is one."

A moth flutters up and lands on my shoulder. I pick it up absentmindedly between my thumb and forefinger and pop it in my mouth, then chew and swallow. I might have access to all kinds of food here in 2018, but I'm not one to turn down nutrition in any form. I need to tell her about Safeco. She has to know to watch her back. But I can't force the words out. Not yet. Instead, I raise my knees to my chest and wrap my arms around my legs in the chilly night air. "Okay, I'm convinced. And thank you for explaining it to me. You're in command here. Please don't think I would ever overstep your authority or challenge you in any way."

It's a very Tower thing to say, and Rosie puts her hand on my shoulder. "Thank you. But Ellen, times are different here, and you're right. I can't keep you in the dark and I don't expect you to jump on my say-so. I value your insight and your opinions. I'll always be honest with you from here on out, and all I can ask is that you do the same."

Is she reading my mind? There will never be a better opening to tell her about Safeco's treachery. I swallow hard. "So what should we do for the next couple of weeks while we're waiting for your dad to get conceived?" What the frack did I just say? I was supposed to confess, to come clean about Safeco and how I ended up here in the first place. I wish I could reach out, snatch the words out of the air and stuff them back in my mouth, but Rosie's already replying.

"That's the trouble," she says. "I have no idea. Until I can start fortifying The Towers, I don't know which way to turn. I'm lost and completely directionless." Her hand flies to her mouth, covering a sharp intake of breath.

"What?" I ask.

"What I just said…it reminded me of something." She clambers to her feet, but I reach up, grab her hand, and pull her back down beside me.

"Rosie, are you honestly planning on going somewhere right now? It's after midnight. If you're worried about your dad finding you, then maybe we shouldn't be the only people walking around on deserted city streets."

"We'll take a bus."

"The buses don't run often at night, and what's to say your dad isn't stalking bus stops, expecting you to show up? We need sleep. We need to wait until the middle of the day, when the streets will be full of people. If you want to do this, we need to be smart about it."

Rosie bows her head and sighs. "You're right. Tomorrow's soon enough. Let's get some sleep."

"Three-hour REM cycle?" I ask. "I'll take the first watch?"

"Agreed."

She crawls into the hollow in the bushes and I follow. She curls up and lays her head on her backpack. "I wish we could see the stars," she says in a quiet voice. "The light from the city is too bright; it blocks them out."

I've never seen them, either. "I'm not sure they exist," I reply.

"Carlos says they do." Rosie wriggles over onto her other side. "Then again," she murmurs, "Carlos said a lot of things that weren't true."

"Sleep well, Rosie."

It's an empty platitude. I know she won't. And neither will I.

One click takes you to FADE TO BLACK!

ABOUT THE AUTHOR

Penelope Wright spent a quarter of her life on the east coast and the rest in Washington state. She worked her way through college in restaurants, hospitals, factories, and everything in between, finally graduating summa cum laude from the University of Washington after an absurdly long time. She loves both traditions and new experiences, and will try anything once, except skydiving, which is a hard no. She lives north of Seattle with her husband and two amazing daughters.

ALSO BY PENELOPE WRIGHT

The Collapse Series:
The Collapse Book One: Time Bomb
The Collapse Book Two: Paradox Rising
The Collapse Book Three: Doomsday Clock
The Collapse Book Four: Five Minutes to Midnight
The Collapse Book Five: Fade to Black
The Collapse Book Six: Conundrum

Stand-alone Books:
No Use for a Name

ACKNOWLEDGMENTS

I've always been fascinated by time travel and all the possibilities it holds, and I've wanted to write it for a very long time but found myself making one false start after another. I thank my critique group, Jennifer Bardsley, Laura Moe, Sharman Badgett-Young, and Louise Cypress, for their invaluable insights and developmental help. This book literally would not exist without them, and I cannot thank them enough.

I'd also like to thank my editor, Amy McNulty, for her sharp eyes and excellent attention to detail. Time travel is a difficult beast, and any errors, mistakes, or – gulp – conundrums are mine and mine alone. Huge thanks goes to Nicole Conway for her gorgeous cover designs which I loved the moment I saw them. An extra special thank you to Jennifer Bardsley, again, for formatting the inside to be just as beautiful as the outside.

I'd like to thank my friends Lindsey Wright and Nathan Beck for beta reading and offering extremely helpful feedback. Additionally, I'd like to thank Lindsey, Nathan, and my friends CarrieAnn Brown and Joie Stevens for being utterly awesome.

Finally, I'd like to thank my husband, Travis Wright, and my daughters, Madeline and Annika, for being the most perfect family I could ever hope for. You're all amazing and interesting people and I'm so lucky you're the ones I get to spend most of my time with.

Made in United States
North Haven, CT
15 November 2021

11166882R00111